CH[illegible]
OF THE
NIGHT

E.SCRILL

CHILDREN OF THE NIGHT

Street Ink Publications

15740 W. 7 Mile #1600

Detroit, MI 48235

http://streetinkbooks.com

Special thanks to Sylvia Hubbard for her assistance with the typesetting of this novel. Street Ink sends an even bigger shout out to the people of Detroit who believed in and supported us!

Chapter 1

John Dollar watched with train-wreck awe as his nerdy-looking opponent gracefully sank three consecutive balls before dropping the eight.

At a hundred seventy-five pounds, Johnny stood five-ten with sandy-brown skin, had braids that touched his shoulders, and a hair-trigger temper. Loving to inflict pain, his pockets were kept fat by the many street players and ghetto paper folders who had been excessively pissed off or had monetary losses that needed recouping.

Johnny preferred working with a blade or his bare hands, bringing his homie Ross along anytime gun play was involved. He was proficient with a gun, but got a greater sense of accomplishment if he was blessed with an opportunity to actually feel a jugular vein depress under his palm. He was a wanton killer, and was once told by his tenth-grade art teacher that he was a helluva painter. He failed the assignment anyway because contrary to his teacher's instructions, every person in his paintings had their eyes closed, dead, like he wanted them to be.

Though his friends were scarce, the women in his life weren't. With a reputation for keeping his pockets full, he would usually have two or three bitches on his line at a time...if they managed to put up with his stormy sex.

After smashing Johnny in all three games of pool, the nerd looked to him and gave a told-ya-so smile that invited Johnny's willing hands to the nerd's strangle-ready throat.

As much as he loved puttin' the hurt on fools, he passed, knowing the doomsday gorillas who worked as bouncers were strategically planted throughout the grimy afterhour, and wouldn't stop after pulling him off the nerd, but would also stomp his guts out, then fleece him for his cash and shiny possessions.

Fearing that the nerd would still be doing something punishable by death, Johnny dropped a crumpled hundred onto the green and walked away. Heading for the dice table, he got a feeling of castrating dread as he noticed his younger cousin, Derek, over at the crap tables grandstanding with Smurf's cash.

Smurf was a local heavyweight in the weed game. He would front Derek twenty or thirty pounds every two weeks. If Derek ran through those, he could come back for as many as he needed as long as he paid his ticket. Smurf was blue-black, short as celebrity marriages, and Godzilla ballin'. Niggas would kill just to get the chance to work for him.

Johnny never liked the fact that his cousin worked for Smurf. Derek wasn't at all responsible, but could hustle his ass off. He was tall and lanky and always felt like he had something to prove.

"Nigga, this twenty gees'," Derek began, holding his pocket's entire contents in both hands. "I ain't pressed about that ho-ass two hundred that's on the table, but you ain't catch the dice!"

Johnny watched as the sea of eyes that surrounded the crap table all focused on Derek. Johnny was almost certain that Derek had stopped to leave the cash at his house, but must have changed his mind thinking of all the broads he could flex in front of. *This dumb mu'fucka!* Johnny thought as Derek's display pulled the plug on the argument, but had every lick-hitter in the joint watching with cash-induced murder on the brain.

The snake-faced dice-catcher tossed Derek the ivory cubes. "Yo' dice. Shoot two hun."

Johnny kept his distance, watching Derek's back while allowing him to seem alone.

After Derek won a thousand, Johnny followed him into the next room where couples sweated on the dancefloor and flesh peddling titty-dancers rode a brass pole atop the freak stage.

"You ready?" Johnny asked.

"Not yet. I'm tryin' to find somethin' loose to drag up to one of them rooms," Derek replied with an eighty-proof slur, referring to the VIP rooms on the upper level which were rented for fifty dollars at thirty minute intervals.

Johnny scoped out the exits, planning an escape to avoid getting stuck like a postage stamp. "Look, playa, we gotta raise up. I got Sonya waitin' for me at the apartment."

Derek followed reluctantly as Johnny sliced through the crowded room toward the exit.

Outside, the sun still slept, and a cool morning breeze refrigerated Johnny's perspiring forehead as he strolled toward the parking lot. "Man, that was some dumb-ass shit you did in there," he told Derek.

"Aw, that wasn't nothing, man. Them niggas know who I am."

"What the fuck is that s'posed to mean? That they won't kill you?"

They shuffled toward the parking lot and passed a chubby

guy with his hands in his pockets, standing at the bus stop. As they reached the end of the building and turned to the mouth of the parking lot, they were met by snake-face, slinking from the shadows behind a dumpster, holding a .44 caliber ghost-maker.

"Y'all know what this is! Get y'all asses over here on the ground!"

Johnny's thoughts of making a getaway were smothered by the shadow of the chubby man from the bus stop, coming up behind, brandishing the makings of a bad day.

Snake-face stepped to the side to allow them room to kiss the pavement. As snake-face ran Johnny's pockets, Johnny could hear Derek take a foot to the ribs. He was glad Derek was made to suffer since everything was his fault. Johnny hated to part with his Jacob watch, but played possum for chalk outline prevention.

"Respect me, nigga!" snake-face yelled as he and chubby bent the corner like track stars.

Johnny rose to his feet, watching as Derek whined on and on about losing Smurf's cash. Johnny wasn't scared, just pissed off. He knew a beef was in the forecast, and knew Smurf had an army ready to smash fools like Derek. Even though Johnny knew Derek had fucked up, he wasn't about to let his peeps go out like that. Not when he himself was the headbuster who helped Detroit's murder rate reach skyscraping highs.

The shit was on the flo'!

Chapter 2

Johnny watched as Derek paused before getting out of the car. He knew what Derek wanted, but wasn't trying to hear it.

"Hey, man, why don't you just lend me the dough to pay Smurf," Derek began with shaken words. "You know I'll throw it back to you. I know you got it, dog."

"What you mean, you know I got it? It don't matter if I got it or not, you had it but jacked it off. You think I'm gon' slide you more loot to jack off?"

"You the one that wanted to go in there."

"Yeah for a couple games of pool. Not to flex another nigga's dough or get my trick on. You said them niggas know you, so Smurf should know you, too!"

"Man, damn!" Derek reached for the door handle allowing his slow, hesitant movements to affirm his unfortunate calamity.

Johnny laughed to himself as he watched Derek drag his feet walking to his front door. Derek was looking to the ground as if he would find the cash in his path.

Johnny knew what he intended to do to help Derek, but wasn't going to give Derek the relief of knowing he would get help; he was going to lose some hair as well as sleep over this one. Johnny knew that if he did let Derek know what was going to go down, Derek would find some way to screw up the plans and possibly put them both in an ocean of quicksand.

Johnny headed for his apartment where he knew his woman, Sonya, would be waiting with amorous stress relief. His foot sank the gas pedal and his dick got hard thinking of lifting Sonya's nightgown to sink into her Creole creaminess. He whipped into his parking lot, ignored the speed bumps and skidded into his spot under the shelter. He then pranced through the front door.

Yanking off his jacket, he started through the dark living room, for the bedroom, for Sonya. His enchanted thoughts were cut short when he tripped over what felt like a person.

"Shhh, be quiet, Johnny," Sonya's voice said.

"What the fuck is goin' on?" he whispered. "What you doin' out here on the floor?"

"Don't you remember a few days ago when I told you that some of my family would probably be staying here if they came to town? You know Hurricane Katrina tore Louisiana up, and I ain't 'bout to have my people stayin' in no stadium."

"So what, we got to sleep on the floor till they fix up Louisiana?"

"Naw. I just let them get the bed tonight so they can relax some. Think about how long they been on the road comin' here. You would want a soft bed to relax in for at least one night, wouldn't you?"

Johnny looked around rubbing his chin. He didn't really care about the whole situation, but knew he should maybe try to fake some sort of sympathy. If he didn't, he knew Sonya would be mad and just lie still when he got ready to fuck, then the sex would be empty. She would never refuse his advances, knowing he would rough her off anyway. But he still hated when the sex was empty.

A few months after he and Sonya first got together, they had a big falling out over some broad that Johnny used to screw around with. They saw his old flame in the mall, and she treated him like he was some sort of celebrity. She rushed over, ignoring Sonya, jumping all up in his face. Handing him her business card, the dizzy broad began bragging about getting her real estate license.

Sonya's face was rage-red, and she instantly cut into him about taking the business card. But her tongue got way too sharp and was soon silenced by a vicious back-hand in the middle of the mall.

After a quiet ride home, Johnny ate, then joined Sonya in the bed. He never even thought to apologize before he reached over and grabbed her leg. Her fury was obvious when she pulled away and turned her back to him. Johnny reached over again, grabbing her legs, flipping her over onto her back, grabbing the waist ban of her panties, lifting her lower half into the air with the panties passing over her legs. Johnny got a kick to the chest, but froze her resistance with an arctic stare before ripping her legs apart and forcing himself into her dry womb. As she lay there like a mannequin, he began humping with violent force, gripping her ass, pulling her toward him with every stroke until she began sounding off as he pumped.

"So who's in the bed?" he asked as he sat on the couch to rcmovc his shocs.

"Gwen, my younger sister and Mona, my cousin. My mother, grandma, and auntie stayed with my uncle down in Texas. They didn't feel like making the long trip."

"But, I guess lil' sis' and 'em wanted to see what the D was all about, huh?"

"Yeah, I guess so. So where you been all night?"

"Fuckin' 'round with Derek's dumb ass. That fool got us robbed at the afterhour."

"Awww," she sing-songed with affectionate pity, rubbing her warm hand up Johnny's leg. "I can make you feel better if you promise to keep quiet; my sister was always the nosy type."

Johnny felt his dick rise as he pulled his shirt over his head and tossed it onto the couch. After kicking his boxers onto the heap of clothes, he reached for the remote to the stereo system and turned to the jazz station, mostly for low noise to veil any sex sounds, knowing things were bound to get heated.

Johnny crept with cat-burgling stealth, joining his lady under the cozy comforter, mimicking his old-school game when he had to smuggle chicks into granddaddy's basement to the sneak-a-freak room.

His eyes bulged with lust as he reached for Sonya's night gown but touched her soft skin instead. He dropped his mouth to one of her perky nipples and suckled like a famished infant.

"Ooohh," she purred, lifting his chin with her forefinger so that their eyes met. "Come on, I'm already wet; I been waiting for you all night!" she said as a smile registered on her face.

At that moment, Johnny didn't care if they were on the floor, on the moon, or at the bottom of the sea. He felt fingernails glide up his back as he slid into her heated swamp. As Johnny stroked with relentless abandon, all stress, worry, and upcoming issues were washed away by Sonya's love.

* * *

Johnny woke to the smell of ham and eggs cooking. Still wrapped in the comforter, he turned to the direction of the kitchen and spied Sonya, working diligently over the stove, cocooned in a fluffy white robe with a scarf over her head. He smiled with naughty thoughts of the night before dancing around in his head. He slithered from under the quilt, crawling on his hands and knees at first, then elevating to his tip-toes as he stalked his prey. His limp member swayed with each step as he neared the stove. His adrenaline flowed like the Nile as his bare feet finally inched across the cold kitchen floor tiles.

Johnny seized the fluffy robe in a bear-hug and moved to smother her cheek with kisses as his dick dangled against her ass.

"Hey!" came a voice from the cocoon. A voice that wasn't Sonya's.

Oh shit! This ain't Sonya! Damn, I forgot all about her family, Johnny thought as he continued to cling to the robe. He was hesitant to release her knowing that as he turned to flee, she would get a glimpse of his naked ass. He knew that keeping his arms around her would only make the violation more severe, so he turned and bolted into the bedroom. After crashing through the door, he was greeted by a curvaceous, panty-wearing fox trying to cover her mesmerizing c-cups with her too little hands as she shrieked like a smoke-filled fire alarm.

"Oh, sorry," Johnny said as while turning, covering his privates, to find asylum elsewhere. He sprinted toward the front door, but thought of his nude state.

The comforter! he remembered as he dove for his small pallet on the floor. He buried himself completely as his heart threw a tantrum.

He couldn't believe he met the other side for the first time while he was completely naked. It wouldn't have been so bad if they were people he would never have to encounter again, but these were his woman's people.

Johnny could feel the covers shake as he giggled to himself thinking how crazy he must've looked running around naked. He could hear footsteps nearing him, coming from the kitchen and bedroom, but was too ashamed to uncover his face to properly meet Sonya's family. *Where the fuck is Sonya?* He thought, figuring things would be a lot easier if she were there to broker him into their fold.

"Uh, excuse me," a female voice began. "It's no use coverin' up now."

Johnny burst out laughing, then heard the two women laugh. He slowly pulled back the cover and was speechless as he looked at Sonya's double, cocooned in the robe.

He glued his eyes to her, not caring about how rude he may

be, needing to see her lips move with another voice coming out.

"Are you okay?" she asked, revealing a twisted lateral incisor that showed him for sure that she wasn't his woman. But the voice was what released him, so he turned to the shorter female, who was obviously Mona, the cousin.

The sight of Mona's tiggle-bitties was carved into his mind. Even with her now wearing a loose-fitting shirt, he still saw those mesmerizing c-cups.

Johnny couldn't help but blush as he tried to find the right words. "How's it goin', ladies?" he finally mustered before feeling like an even bigger idiot as the two women just laughed.

"Hi, I'm Mona."

"And I'm Gwen. So, I guess that would make you Johnny, huh?"

"Yup, I'm Johnny. Listen I apologize, Gwen, for grabbing you like that."

"What? He grabbed you?" Mona asked in a sarcastic tone. "He only flashed me."

Johnny felt himself blush again. "I thought you was Sonya. Y'all look just alike, damn!"

"Yeah, I hear that all the time about my big sis'. Oh yeah, she ran to the store for some juice and bread. Would you like a few minutes to get yourself together, bro'-in-law?"

"Fo' sho'! Sonya would kill me if she caught me in here naked with two women...even if y'all are her family." Johnny stood with the comforter still wrapped around him and walked into the bedroom while the two women went for the kitchen.

Johnny walked out to the living room after twenty minutes and saw that Sonya had returned. She was sitting on the couch with her legs crossed and eyebrows raised.

"So you been in here showin' off, huh?" Sonya questioned.

Johnny blushed again.

"Don't be smilin'. I'm for real. What you doin' runnin' up on my little sister with yo' dick out? You know I don't share...not even with my family."

"Don't even try it," Johnny began. "You know I thought she was you. You ain't tell me you had a twin."

"We ain't twins. I'm ten months older than her. So what about you runnin' in the room while Mona was dressin'? You thought she was me, too?"

Johnny knew Sonya was just joking with him, but still answered her truthfully. He knew she was well aware that he would tap that ass if she started trippin', but he played along to let her have her glorious moment in front of her kinfolks. "Man, I really forgot they was here. You know how I am when I first wake up."

"Oh, you forgot, huh? Why did you think you was out here on the floor?"

"Yeah, you right. But, you know I was just lookin' for you," he said as he walked over and pecked Sonya's cheek.

"Alright. Don't get hurt up in here," Sonya said as she turned flesh-hungry eyes to him and returned the kiss before leading him to the table where they joined Gwen and Mona for breakfast.

Everything on the table looked picture-perfect like shots on a menu at a classy restaurant, but Johnny could only think of the seductive looks Sonya was giving him, making him think he was to be rewarded for allowing her to shine in front of her peeps.

Ten minutes into breakfast, Johnny's cellphone rang. It was Ross, ready to share the plan he etched together to bring Stone's absconding worker out of hiding.

Stone was the man when it came to heroin. He had an Israeli plug who would drop him a backpack filled with mushroom-shaped chunks of pure dope. Each chunk weighed about thirty grams and was so potent that Stone could stomp it twelve times and still cause a fiend to nod off in the middle of singing the National Anthem. Stone would usually only put a dime on his bag, and as a result set new highs for dope tolerance amongst the veteran junkies. Rookies and out-of-towners who had enough juice to get a taste of Stone's diesel, never knew what hit them until the answer foamed from their mouths.

“When you wanna get together?” Ross asked Johnny.

“Gimme 'bout a hour, then fall through.”

Johnny knew Ross would be outside waiting after about forty-minutes.

At five-six, Ross was so skinny he looked like he could run his arm through his beltloops. He had braids that refused to grow and barely hung past his rear hairline. He was always down to pull a caper, and seemed to come up with the most inventive schemes. Ross didn't lay niggas down for the same reasons Johnny did. Ross just didn't give a fuck. He was wild as a motorcycle club on New Years Eve, and could strategize with the brilliance of a military leader.

Johnny wolfed his food, then hit the cupboard for a few shots of gin. He knew the day was going to be off the hook, especially since Ross had some new mufflers for his pistols that he couldn't wait to use.

Chapter 3

Elisa Benoit sashayed to the salad bar with floozy trashiness. She smirked thinking of her target's unawareness.

She had come to Atlanta in search of an old client, Patrick Brown, who had once fascinated her to the point of fanatical eroticism.

A year and a half ago, Patrick had come to seek out her hex casting abilities to lift him from his financial crawl back to the glitzy hornet of a businessman he once was when his construction business was flourishing. His competition, Upshaw Builders, was puttin' the squeeze on him. Mainly because Stephen Upshaw, the company's owner, was engaged to the daughter of Georgia's governor. Stephen had the juice to get first dibs on all the new contracts, and was starving all other developers in the state of Georgia.

Patrick made the trek to the Louisiana sticks, just outside Baton Rogue, to make a merciful plea to the dark mistress of voodoo.

Patrick found the voluptuous widow, and after his initial consultation discovered that her prices were way too steep for his crumbling pockets, so he toyed with her desolate social state, enriching her barren love life.

He admitted up front that he had no means of paying her steep ticket, but she gunned for the stranger with the Denzel face. She had many clients, but no one for the bump-and-grind. It seemed that no one would chance a relationship with a woman known to practice witchcraft, especially with the unnerving rumors floating around about the deaths of the men in her family.

Over the next two days, Elisa sent poetry and provocative letters to Patrick's motel room, claiming to be possessed by his sexiness. She trashed her scarf for a feathered do.

Patrick decided to play the game, so he popped up at her doorstep with a fistful of freshly cut flowers, overthrowing her washed-up and undesirable feelings with soothing compliments. He took her for quality strolls through the rural countryside, securing her romantically.

Elisa wondered if Patrick was leading her on, but was falling so hard for the city-slicker that she dared not interrupt the youthful, beautiful and wanted way he made her feel.

Patrick watched as Elisa walked her last client out the door, told her how he had found something so special in her that he no longer worried about his troubles back home, that he wanted her for her. He then walked her out back and gave her a dose of knee-buckling sex against a pecan tree, under a full moon, to the croaking chorus of tree frogs.

The next two weeks was a blizzard of daydreamy sex and passionate quality time. He had her feeling like the bad bitch she was when her daughter, Mona's, late father would walk three miles to get the ass. Elisa knew that once Patrick was gone she would be lonely again, so she begged him to relocate and start fresh with her in Louisiana, but he refused, confessing to her about his wife back home. He swore to her that his marriage was dead and that he would soon be free to send for her so that they could continue their blissful romance, but he first had to get his business flowing again and would soon have to leave.

Realizing that she couldn't persuade him to change his mind, she chose to leave a lasting impression by helping him in his economic situation. The day before Patrick dipped, Elisa gave him a fruit preserves jar filled with a jelly-like substance that wasn't fruit preserves. The top layer was red, the middle blue, and the bottom was orange. No matter how Patrick shook or turned the jar, the colors wouldn't mix, and stayed in their zones. Patrick was instructed to place the jar in the crawlspace underneath his competitor's home and his problems would be solved. As Patrick left Elisa for the last time, she kissed him tenderly and handed him a small gri-gri bag that she said would bring him an extra advantage if he kept it in the desk drawer of his office.

For a week after Hurricane Katrina hit Louisiana, Elisa had been stalking Ameka Brown, Patrick's wife, and had followed her and her girlfriends to the small restaurant were they broke for lunch.

Elisa twisted a small pin between her forefinger and thumb. Specially treated, the pin poked through three small paper squares. The first square, which was near the head of the pin, represented Patrick. The second represented Elisa, and the third, Ameka. That was supposed to keep Ameka from coming between Patrick and Elisa.

Elisa grabbed a plate from the cart at the end of the salad bar, then stuck the pin into Ameka's sweater as she closely brushed past her.

Later that evening, Elisa pulled into the driveway of Patrick's Marrietta home. She rang his doorbell several times before he finally peeked through the door. He looked nervous as a guppy in a tank full of piranha's. He slowly pushed the door open.

“Hey, Mrs. Benoit. How can I help you?” he asked.

Elisa snatched the screen door open, then pushed past

Patrick. She looked to Patrick's hand as he grabbed her arm.

"Hold up! Where do you think you're going?" he asked.

"I'm comin' in here to see you, baby," she drawled.

"What the fuck do you mean?" he began in a loud whisper. "I live here with my wife. You know that!"

"You don't have to worry about her," Elisa said with an extra sneaky look on her face.

"What?" Patrick said as a horrified look washed over his face. He dashed out of his living room, sprinting through the house calling his wife's name, but got no answer.

Elisa casually strutted through the house behind Patrick turning down any pictures that had Ameka in them. She flexed an evil grin as Patrick seized her by the shoulders and hollered, "What did you do with my wife? She was just in here a minute ago!"

Elisa calmly patted one of Patrick's arms. "Calm down, dear. I think she went out for a while. What makes you think I did something with her anyway?" Elisa asked as she looked into Patrick's face with teasing sarcasm.

He released Elisa, and as he tried to calm himself he said, "Elisa, please, my wife has nothing to do with us not being together. Please tell me where she is. Please!"

"You're still in love with her, aren't you?"

"She's my wife. What do you expect?"

"You wasn't actin' like that when you needed me!"

"I'm sorry if I led you on. You have to understand...I was desperate."

"Oh, so you decided to use your good looks and smooth charm to get what you wanted. Where does that leave me?"

"I—I.."

"Save it! So, I hear your business is doing well again," she said with extorting suggestiveness.

"Look, I'll pay you whatever you want, Elisa. Just bring me my wife!"

"From the prices I charge, you should know I got money.

But it ain't no fun to be with you if I got to twist your arm to. You can give me whatever you think is right." Elisa turned and stared out the front window.

Patrick ran to get in front of her, to get her attention. "Look, Elisa, I really didn't know me and my wife were going to patch things up when we were together."

"I told you, save it. Don't worry. I'm not mad, just hurt. I have nothing left; everything I owned got fucked up by the hurricane. You was the only thing I had to look forward to."

"Elisa--"

"I get here to find that I been played!" She captured Patrick with pitiful eyes as tears streamed down her face. "Your wife is in the backyard."

"Just wait here a minute," Patrick said as he scrambled to peek out the back window. He then dashed into his bedroom and came back with his checkbook. "I see the light is on in the garage. Is that where Ameka is?"

"I don't know. I thought I heard her going out the back door when I was coming in," Elisa said, toying with Patrick the way he had with her emotions.

"Here, Elisa, I'm writing you a check for twice as much as you asked for," Patrick said, obviously realizing the dangers of having a vexed voodoo priestess on his ass.

Elisa snatched the check, then turned toward the door.

"Aren't you going to undo whatever you did to my wife?"

"I told you, I ain't do nothin' to her," she smiled deceptively, knowing that Ameka only went out back because she couldn't come between Patrick and Elisa, she couldn't even be in the house at the same time Elisa was there, but as long as Elisa wasn't around, everything would be fine.

As Elisa drove toward her motel, she thought about going to see her mother and sister, but knew it would be drama if she did. They didn't want anything to do with her since she started working with roots and hexes. It was her mother and sister who had to go behind her and undo much of her black magic after her victims found that medical science knew nothing that could save them. They would never tell their clients that it was their family member who had them screwed up, but would just fix them.

Some say the thin veil of skin that covered Elisa's sister's face at birth was what gave her clairvoyance, but their mother in her younger days would've made Elisa seem like a Girl Scout. But after becoming a devout Christian, she changed her ways and hated Elisa for choosing to indulge in the dark arts.

Elisa wasn't very close to her daughter because she was always too strict, and that caused Mona to rebel against her and eventually move in with Elisa's mother. But Elisa knew Mona went to Detroit to be with her cousins and could possibly be feeling home-sick also, so Elisa headed for interstate 75, Detroit-bound, to find someone on the planet who cared.

* * *

Ross sat in his forest-green conversion van rolling a blunt. He knew Johnny would take forever, so he decided to get his high on while he waited. He looked up after lighting the weed and saw two females coming out of the apartments Johnny lived in. He rolled down his window as he watched the ladies walk toward their car.

"Excuse me, can I talk to you for a minute," he asked as he pulled to a space next to their car.

The taller female looked at him for a second before she tossed the keys to the shorter female.

"I see you, girl," the shorter female said.

The taller female looked back and rolled her eyes comically before continuing to the van.

"How you doin'? My name is Ross."

"I'm Gwen."

"Y'all live in there?"

"No. We just here visitin', that's all."

"Oh, okay. Well, I don't see no rings on your hands so I don't think you're married, but do you got a man?"

"No, not right now."

"Well let me give you my number so we can keep in touch."

"I don't know, I'm not from here, and I'm not sure how long I'll be stayin'."

"Well, that's cool. Just hit me up while you're here. Maybe I can show you around some. You sound like you're from down south somewhere."

"Yeah, Louisiana."

"Oh, damn!" he said as he took a pull from the weed. He realized that she cracked a smile when she saw the blunt. "You smoke?" he asked, offering the blunt.

"Of course." After a puff, she exhaled a gust of smoke toward the other female who was still standing outside their car.

The shorter female rushed over. "What's up? Can I get down, too?"

Gwen passed the blunt. "You can give me your number, but I don't have my cellphone anymore."

"Just call me when you can," Ross said.

"I hear ya', girl. Up in here networkin'," said the shorter female after blowing out a mouthful of smoke.

Ross watched as the weed took effect and tried to close the females' eyes.

"This that fire!" said the shorter female. "We ain't got no greens like this back home." Her southern accent became more prevalent and her smile shined between her words.

"Uh-oh, here comes the flasher," Gwen said to the shorter female.

Ross looked up and saw Johnny walking over to the van as the women engaged in a fit of laughter.

"What's up, playa?"

"Oh, you know Johnny?" Gwen asked.

"Yeah, that's my dog. That's who I'm waitin' for. How y'all know him?"

"What? That's bro'-in-law."

Ross looked closely at Gwen. "Damn, you do look like Sonya. That's yo' sister?"

"Yeah. That's who we visitin'."

Johnny hopped into the van with Ross as the ladies walked away.

"Why you ain't tell me you had these women up in there with you, man?"

"You know I don't too much like niggas I know kickin' it wit' my peoples; anytime somethin' go wrong, I get the blame. I ain't have nothin' to do wit' dat. That's y'all."

"Is Gwen cool?"

"Shit, I don't know. I just met 'em today, too! Fuck them right now. Put me up on the layout."

"Ol' boy don't care 'bout getting no money back, right?"

"Right."

"Okay, cool. I know where his worker goes for breakfast every morning. It's a little joint on Six Mile near the Lodge freeway. My cousin got a salon by it and say while that nigga be sittin' in his car waitin' for his food to get ready, he be tryin' to spit game at everything goin' by in a skirt."

"Oh, so he be out in his car waitin' huh?"

"Hell yeah."

"Let's get 'em!"

Chapter 4

Sonya stood behind the bar of the strip club where she worked watching her tip jar overflow as she mixed drink after drink. She had been tending bars for six years and had been at the Bald Monkey for two.

Once she got a break in her orders, she emptied most of her tip jar to make room for more money, then thought of the situation going on at her apartment. She felt good about helping her family, but knew they wouldn't be able to stay in her one-room apartment too much longer, especially with her having her man living with her. She knew Gwen wouldn't play her close, but Mona, that was a different story. Lil' cuz was buck-wild. Mona had already asked if Sonya would mind her coming to the club for a dancing gig. Sonya knew that if Mona did, she would have to keep them being related a secret, because somehow, someway, Mona would do something to cost Sonya her job.

She was glad she had kept her relationship with Johnny

secret when he was a bouncer, because when the new owner took over a year ago, he was fired for not splitting the money he made taxing people to sit in the booths with the house. Johnny used to make a killin' charging for the high-rise booths since it was so hard to distinguish between a lap dance and actual sex if a guy was in one. Whoever sat in the booth with him would all get out and stand in front of the booth, blocking the view from the rest of the bar, allowing their dog to get his trick on.

If they knew Sonya was Johnny's lady, the new Italian bosses would've found a reason to fire her, too.

Sonya thought of Mona's ex, and wondered if their family was really cursed like everyone used to say. Before she could finish that thought, she looked up. *Aw, hell-to-the-naw! Is that Aunt Lisa?* Sonya thought as she watched Elisa push through the crowded bar. "Hey, Auntie!"

"Hey, baby. So this is where you make all that money?"

"Yeah, whatever. You seen your daughter?"

"Naw, not yet. Where is she? Gwen said they was comin' up here today."

"She did? I ain't know they was comin' here today. Not that it matters."

"So you gonna get Mona a job in here?"

"Now, Auntie, you know I don't mind lookin' out for my family, but your daughter is wild as hell!"

"I hear ya, girl."

"But, I did tell her about amateur night tomorrow. All she gotta do is be here with her costume at eight and kick it with the manager."

"Oh, okay. That shouldn't be too hard."

"Auntie, just between me and you, what happened to her boyfriend?"

"Aw, that was bad. He was a real nice young man, too. I guess them other guys down home new he was sellin' dope and knew he would have all his money with him when he left."

"Uh, huh," Sonya said as she listened closely.

"They crashed into his truck before he could get on the freeway, and when he got out to exchange info with them, they just shot him."

"Damn!"

"Yeah, girl. I'm glad they didn't hurt Mona. They took all his stuff, the clothes, money, jewelry, everything. Them jokers is dirty down there. I liked him so much, too, because he really cared about Mona. She wouldn't even have to get a job if he was still around. That boy did everything for her. He sold drugs, but he was a good man, you know what I mean?"

"Yeah, I hear you." Sonya's thoughts went to Johnny. How he would always try to make her happy. She knew he wasn't as empathetic as guys in most other relationships, but still tried to make things work and keep a smile on her face. There were rare occasions when Sonya dined on knuckle sandwiches, but she couldn't see herself without him.

"What's wrong, baby?" Elisa asked.

"Oh, nothing. I was just thinking. So where you stayin' at?"

"At the Residence Inn in Dearborn. I wanted someplace where I could cook for myself sometimes. I don't know how long it will be before they get things together back home. Well, looks like you got some customers; I'll be checkin' in on ya'." Elisa turned and disappeared into the crowd, leaving Sonya wondering just how things would be with Mona shaking her ass at the bar.

* * *

Amateur night was busy as always at the Bald Monkey. Derek knew Sonya worked at the titty bar, but still came to ease his mind some. He had a thousand in his pocket from his three-grand stash, but since he was short on his ticket anyway, he decided to flex a bit. He knew it was no use just sitting around worrying about his dilemma with Smurf. The Bald Monkey was where a lot of the ballers on the west-side hung at. He figured that he might just run into a line on some dope from somebody else in time to replace Smurf's cash.

Having to pee, Derek ducked into the restroom where Chucky, dressed in a tuxedo shirt with black slacks, manned the sink. Chucky offered liquid soap to those washing their hands, then gave a squirt of lotion along with a breath mint. On the sink's counter sat his small tip basket. Being an entreprenigga, he expanded his hustle, selling mix CD's, pornos, loose blunts, condoms, and other nicknacks. He even had the hook up on pills.

Derek tried to stay out of Sonya's view as he did a lap around the inside of the joint, scoping out all the potentials there for amateur night. The place was packed to the gills with gees, killers, hustlers, lames, and even a few white boys still wearing shirts and ties. With a crowd of this magnitude, it had to be at least fifty gees' worth of single dollar bills ready to be tucked into thongs and garters.

As Derek came back around to where he started, he saw a trick's dream sitting on a barstool. While her thong took refuge between her cheeks like butt-floss, she plucked fries from the basket of some broke-looking character next to her. Derek knew he had never before seen the chick around. Her face was prettier than all the chicks' in the bar. Her figure-eight shape had Derek combing his mind for a line—or even a lie—to put himself at the top of her priority list.

At the DJ's request, the short fox pushed through the platoon of hounds with her pastel come-fuck-me outfit glowing from the luminescent black light that lined the ceiling. She climbed on stage, pumping, grinding, and dancing, seeming to be as agile in stiletto heels as in gym shoes. The stage was being littered with singles as she made her booty clap. The bombshell then grabbed the brass pole in the center of the stage and climbed hand-over-hand to the ceiling. Her jet-black mane dangled as she held the pole between her open legs and slowly slid back down to the stage, bucking her legs along the way as if she were being fucked. She bent over to rake together the blanket of singles with her legs straight, tits hanging, and ass wide as a pony's, sticking out to entice the last-minute flurry of bills.

Derek ordered a shot of Remy VSOP and watched as the chick left the stage and headed to the girl's room.

Derek tried to step up to put his bid in, but got stiff-armed by the goon escorting her.

After regaining his balance, Derek looked back to see the fox going into the girl's room, putting up an index finger, gesturing for him to give her a minute.

Geeked as hell, Derek banged his shot, then ordered a double; he wanted to get his head right so his game would be tight.

When she came out, she had on different clothes, but still had her shorts all up in her ass, looking good enough for Derek to write home about.

"What's up, sexy?" Derek asked.

"Hey," said the short bombshell.

"You can call me D."

"I'm Kitty."

"Is that a dance name or what yo' mama named you?"

"No. My name is Mona. Yo' mama ain't name you D."

"Nope. Derek. You drink?"

"If you buyin'."

Derek flagged a waitress. "Yo, give me a bottle of Moet."

"Black or white label," the waitress asked.

"Aw, man. C'mon, y'all know I like that black label. Nothin' but the best for me and the lady," Derek said, trying to flex in front of Mona. He peeped Sonya out the corner of his eye, shaking her head as she looked his way. *I know Johnny ain't tell her 'bout Smurf. I wonder what she shakin' her head about? Oh, well.*

"You be up in here everyday like the rest of these niggas, don't you?" Mona asked.

"Naw. Just sometimes."

"Good, 'cause I don't usually meet guys where I work."

"Oh, lucky me."

* * *

On the morning of Sweetest Day, Ross and Johnny sat in a beat-down Impala, Ross's bucket, waiting for the right moment to put their target on ice. His name was Cantrell, and he owed Stone twenty thousand dollars that Stone was no longer interested in; he wanted Cantrell dead for playing him close.

As the two faced McNichols and watched from three houses down, Cantrell sat in his grape Hummer, talking shit to a young chick who looked in the face like she'd been hanging out all night. Cantrell sent her into the small eatery they were parked in front of, possibly to get his food or place an order. Ross started the bucket, then slid it into gear. Before they could reach Cantrell, Tony Jack pulled up to the hummer, trying to sell Cantrell some knock-off Gucci bags. Ross crept forward, prepared to ice Tony Jack's hustlin' ass for being in the wrong place.

As soon as Ross cranked his window down, a group of females burst out the small eatery. They had obviously seen Tony Jack's merchandise and wanted in on the goods.

Ross slid his nine back under his seat, then kept on past the crowd of women. They knew they could've let Tony Jack have it with Cantrell, but wasn't about to risk hitting all the women, too.

"Damn, did you see that shit?" Johnny asked.

"Them ho's came outta nowhere. I bet that nigga, Jack is makin' a killin' out there; it's Sweetest Day, too! Shit, I need to sell some purses and shit myself."

"Today is Sweetest Day?"

"Yeah, nigga! You ain't know? Yo' relationship must be on the rocks if you missin' shit like that."

Johnny didn't have a clue as to what type of gifts he should even get on a day like that, but figured that since the women were buggin'-out over the purses, that's what women liked.

"Let me out at the corner."

After Johnny got out, Ross bent the corner and came back to the spot where they were sitting at first. He watched as Johnny got Sonya two purses with matching belts, and wished he had someone to buy something for.

He missed his ex. She was fat and the head was bold, but he still missed her. *Damn, maybe I should get Gwen somethin'. I just met her a few days ago, but I guess it wouldn't hurt,* Ross thought, knowing goodies like that had panty-dropping properties.

Ross pulled into the alley behind the eatery, then hopped out of the car and headed for Cantrell's truck.

As he was walking over, all the ladies left, then Tony Jack left. "Let me check those out, homie," Ross said as he picked up four purses that Cantrell sat down on his hood. "Damn, these fresh as hell! Ol' boy gone, huh?" Ross asked as he looked around.

"Yup," Cantrell said.

Ross bolted toward the alley with the purses. Cantrell gave chase, but couldn't keep up. Ross snatched open the Impala's driver door, hopped in, grabbed his silenced nine-millimeter from under the seat, leaned out, and as Cantrell neared the bucket, Ross strangled three metallic clicks out of his gun. Each click left a red spot on Cantrell's shirt. Cantrell fell forward and slid in the dirt for a foot. Johnny came running up behind him, out of breath, with a giant smile. He hopped into the passenger seat.

"Damn, nigga! Why you ain't tell me you was gon' plug him right then?" asked Johnny.

"Wasn't like I planned it or somethin'; it just went down like that," Ross said as they continued through the alley, coming out on the next street over.

"Well, time to get paid."

Ross turned to Johnny and flashed his teeth. He had four purses for his new friend, and his split for the hit was six gees'.

He wasn't doing too bad for a Saturday, and it wasn't even noon yet.

Chapter 5

Elisa sat at the bar of the Motor City Casino, sipping cosmopolitans, watching the house band perform "Mind Blowing Decisions". She only came to get out of her hotel room. She knew she wouldn't see any of her family since it was Sweetest Day, and the girls would more than likely have someone by now to spend the day with.

She knew Mona was at the bar working with Sonya, and knew if she kept showing up there, Mona might begin to feel uncomfortable.

"Anybody sitting here?" a deep voice asked.

Elisa looked up to see a bald, dark-skinned man in a blue suit with a rose in his hand. "Be my guest." His Perry Ellis cologne had her wanting to hop onto his lap.

"For you," he said as he handed her the rose.

"How is this for me? You don't even know."

"Well, I'm Herb, and you sitting here looking like you could use a friend. So do I have to know you to make you smile?"

"I guess not. I'm Elisa. Thanks; that's very sweet."

"That's what it's all about. You know what today is. So, where's your sweetie?"

"I guess I'm unfortunate this year. I'm from Louisiana and we don't even have Sweetest Day down there, but we need to get it."

"So, you lose your money yet?"

"No. I don't gamble; don't even know how."

"Come with me to the blackjack table. Watch me play a few hands, then get in if you pick up on the game."

"You don't want me and my bad luck with you. You better go without me."

"You lookin' too good to give me bad luck. If I lose all my money, I still win as long as you with me." Elisa followed as Herb confidently turned and headed for the tables.

She watched as Herb split two aces, then received a face card for each one.

"Blackjack! Blackjack! I told you I wasn't gonna have bad luck with you. I need you with me all the time!"

Yeah, that's what you sayin' now, she thought, knowing she had a chance to get to know Herb as long as he didn't find out what she did for a living.

After winning seven out of ten hands, Herb stood from the table. "You want to get something to eat or something? I feel like the least I could do is feed you since you brought me all this luck and everything."

Elisa thought for a long moment, then gave Herb the silk to spin her web for her. "I'm tired of being around all these people; I guess I'm just a country girl."

"Well, ain't nothin' wrong with that. I just won eight hundred bucks. We should celebrate together. How about gettin' some room service at my room overlookin' downtown Detroit?"

"Why you tryin' to take me to a room? You married?"

"No, I'm single, but since we been havin' so much fun, why not go chill and enjoy the view while we sip champagne?"

Elisa sat and listened to Herb's bid for her company. He was handsome and charming, but his being forward is what turned her on the most. She was ready to bounce, but decided to hold out for a few minutes longer, just so she wouldn't seem as eager as she was. "You never even told me what you do for a living. You could be a killer for all I know."

"Aww, c'mon now! Do I look like a killer to you? I work for the labor union at a auto plant."

"Auto plant? I thought you might've been some kind of businessman."

"Is that the kind of men you like? Do I need to be in business to get your company?"

"No. You're fine."

"I just like to dress when I go out."

And I like a man who likes to dress! "Now see, I really don't believe you single now."

"I am! Just been waitin' for the right person, that's all. I don't want to be with somebody that just want me 'cause I got a decent job."

"How you know I don't?"

"You might, but since we start havin' so much fun before you even knew who I was..." With the spunk of a high school athlete on prom night, he threw his arm around the shapely sorceress and started for the door, for her web. Elisa snuggled close, loving Herb's cockiness as her arm went around his waist and more of his cologne went up her nostrils.

* * *

"Is that all you want to eat?" Derek asked Mona as they ordered a meal at Seldom Blues.

She wanted to go all out since he was paying, but opted to keep her figure tight for her new dancing gig. "I don't eat a lot. You know you wouldn't want me if I was fat."

"I don't know; you clean up pretty damned nice. You look like a black Cinderella in that dress," Derek said with an intrigued look.

I hate when he stare at me like that! Mona thought, knowing she had him open from the first time she rode his dick. For the past three days they had been busy wearing out the springs in his mattress, but she knew she would soon cut him off once she found something better. She liked his company, but he was too soft for her and she hated that. She liked the type of guy who would just roll over on her, not the type who felt like he needed to ask first.

She liked the way he spoiled her, though, and hoped his cash would last. She didn't think he actually had the kind of cash he tried to make her think he did. She knew his type all too well, could smell them the way dogs could smell fear in a human. The type that would always break themselves trying to buy love. That type always seemed to irritate her when they weren't spending, but she didn't want to be alone too much after the death of her fiancée. He was dead and still had her heart.

"Is that your cellphone vibratin'?" she asked, seeing that he was obviously trying to ignore it.

"Yeah, let me see who this is right quick." He hesitated when he saw the number.

"What's wrong? I don't care if it's a woman. Gone on and answer it," she said teasingly while hoping it was another chick so she wouldn't look so bad when guys started calling her.

"Aw, naw, that ain't it. I just told all them fools not to bother me while I spend time with you today. Hold up."

She watched as Derek tried to twist his body to keep her from hearing.

"Hello," he said.

Mona tried to look busy going through her purse, but could hear someone shout over the line, "Nigga, where the fuck you been? Where the fuck is my loot?"

"Oh, man, you know I got you," Derek began. "I got a few more dollars I got to pick up in the streets and I'll get right at you." Mona happened to look up as Derek slid his finger over and pressed the off button. "Dog, don't be rushin' me! I told you not to call me today anyway."

No this nigga ain't frontin'!

After eating, Derek stood and hugged Mona. She could feel something in his pocket pressing against her leg and hoped it was a gift, so she allowed him to take her back to his house again.

Soft music played as Mona sipped on the Remy Derek had waiting. Trying to think of the fastest way into his pocket, she stripped down to her panties and bra, then reached for his zipper. He slowly spun her around and held her from behind. She could feel him slip his hand into his pocket.

"This is for you," he said as he fastened a diamond tennis bracelet around her wrist. "Happy Sweetest Day."

I hope this nigga don't get his head busted tryin' to impress me; I would feel so bad. I'm keepin' this bitch, though! "I feel bad 'cause I don't have nothin' to give you."

He turned her back around. After hearing his zipper, she allowed him to move her hand to his stiffness.

"Fix this for me," he asked with a nervous look on his face.

I know this lame ain't pressin' his luck like that! "You mean suck it?"

"Yeah, what's wrong with that? You sayin' you ain't never did it before?"

Mona froze her blush over and twisted her face and tilted her head to the indignant position. With her lethal mouth aimed at his head, she loaded her tongue with backbone-piercing cusswords and prepared to verbally execute him. "Here, you can take this bullshittin' bracelet back if you think I'm gon' suck yo' dick for it!" she said in a stank way, knowing she wanted to keep it, but had to let the lame know what time it was. She was a vet when it came to giving head, but wasn't about to serve Derek up like a king when he carried himself like a peon. “I'm savin' that for my wedding night anyway!”

“I can understand that. Just keep the bracelet, please. I ain't mean to offend you or nothin', I was just askin'.”

“Did I ever ask you for anything? See, y'all niggas ain't shit!”

“Mona, why don't you chill? Let's cool out and watch a movie or somethin'; it's Sweetest Day. Ain't no point in us fallin' out.”

“I don't want us to fall out, either, but you know you wrong. That's tryin' to play me like a ho. You shoulda just put it up front when you met me if you only wanted to trick. At least then I woulda knew how to handle the situation. All up in here frontin' like you catchin' feelin's for me! See, man, just take me home!” she said, just making sure she had him in check.

“Please just wait for a minute, okay? Let's kill this Remy I got here, then I'll take you home if you still want to go. Cool?” he bargained.

“Man, fuck you!” she said, doggin' him since he punked out when she pulled his card. “You ain't even apologize to me. Give me my dress!”

“Okay! I'm sorry!”

* * *

After the Cantrell hit, Ross stashed his bucket in a parking garage and switched back to his van. He and Johnny drove to see Stone, got paid, then went to Johnny's apartment to scoop their ladies.

Ross marveled at the resemblance Gwen had to Sonya. He thought she looked a lot better, though.

“Hey, Gwen,” Ross began. “I know I said I would only be a hour, but we got a little held up. So, we still hangin' out?”

“Yeah, I guess so.”

“You wanna get a room downtown?”

“A room? And what makes you think I'm ready for all that? I ain't even been talkin' to you for a week yet.”

"Well, that's where I'm goin'. You can come if you want." Ross knew that Gwen liked him, but didn't want to give up her goods too soon. He figured she would have to make an exception since that day was special. He could tell she was a good girl, more like an old-fashioned country girl trying to be down. Which was good seeing how all the city girls only recognized bling and big rims or were dykey. Ross knew Gwen would be a lot easier to deal with once he dropped her gifts on her.

Johnny called Ross into the bathroom. "Hey, dog, what y'all gettin' into tonight? I can't think of nowhere to take my girl. The concerts all sold out, the movies don't seem good enough for today, and dinner by itself ain't enough."

"I'm 'bout to drag ol' girl to the room."

"She gon' let you fuck already?"

"She can make up her mind when we get there, but we goin'."

"She ain't like Sonya said Mona is; you got the good girl. You might have to date six months, go to church, and meet the parents before you can tap that."

"Well, once we get to our room at the Westin overlookin' downtown, and these fresh purses I got have her ass smilin', I'll spit some of this Fenkell-Ave game in her ear. Then, she can decide whether or not I can get that soon-to-be-drunk pussy. I think I got a helluva chance, what about you?"

"I can't argue with that. Name y'all first two kids after me," Johnny laughed, then slapped palms with Ross. "Shit, I think that's what I'm gon' do, too. I got this thang to do for Ken as soon as he give me the address, then just grab one of them rooms down there and lay up with my breezy."

"Let me know if you need me tonight; I'm ready!" Ross said.

After the couples checked in and were walking through the hotel lobby, Johnny's cellphone rang. "Hello?"

Ross could tell by the look on Johnny's face that it was time to put in more work.

"Sonya, I need you to drop me and Ross off at the casino."

"Right now?" she asked, looking as if she wanted to slap him.

"Yeah, baby. I promise I won't be long. I promise."

"That's okay. Just make sure you bring me a shrimp and crab salad from the casino deli or you ain't gettin' in the room."

"Deal!"

Ross didn't even ask, knowing it had to be something major if Johnny was leaving Sonya at the room on a night like that. To cover his own ass, he took Gwen's purses out of his overnight bag and set them on the bed so she could see them and be ready for him when he returned.

After being dropped off on Grand River in front of the casino, Ross followed Johnny to the gas station.

"That was Ken that called," Johnny began. "He said that Carlos off Biltmore was his brother, Chuck's bunky in the county jail while Chuck was fightin' that domestic violence case. He said Chuck beat the domestic violence, but got five years for witness tampering."

"I thought Carlos was doin' four years?"

"Me too. Evidently, he been in the county workin' that shit off. He went through Chuck's mail and found a letter Chuck was gon' send to his old lady, and gave it to one of the deputies. That's how they got Chuck. Now Carlos is out after doin' six months."

"I thought that nigga, Carlos was hard core."

"He is with a gun. Ain't no guns in the joint, though." Johnny bought two sodas in glass bottles, a gas can, a small bottle of dish detergent, and paid for two dollars worth of gas. They then headed for the Jeffries projects where Carlos was layin' low.

In the shadow of a dumpster, Ross watched as Johnny took off his shoes and socks. He put his shoes back on, then put his socks on his hands like gloves. He poured out the sodas, then put an inch of detergent in the bottles. He tossed the rest of the detergent into the dumpster, then filled the bottles up three-quarters of the way with gas before flinging the gas can into the dumpster. Johnny took off the socks, then jammed them into the bottles.

"Go to the back of the building and light the socks, then throw them through the window," Johnny told Ross.

Ross gave Johnny a few minutes to get to the front of the building. He sparked the socks, then threw the first bottle hard enough for it to collide with the wall on the inside of the dwelling. He tossed the second through the next window which was another room in the same unit. He was amazed at how fast the flames spread through the small unit. For a minute, he stood in a trance until he heard voices coming from inside headed for the front of the unit. He dashed around to help Johnny.

When Ross caught up with Johnny, Johnny was pulling his knife out of a body. Ross looked around to see two more bodies laying in pools of blood. They turned and ran back to the casino. They hopped on the Grand River bus and went to spend Sweetest Day with their ladies.

Chapter 6

"Ooohh yeah, baby take it off," Herb told Elisa as she danced erotically.

As she performed the appetizing strip tease, she allowed the downtown skyline to serve as a backdrop for the freak-show. Herb was making her feel so wanted again, letting her know she didn't have to settle for just anything and could still reel in a nice catch.

Down to her lace panties and bra, she put the show on hold. "Give me a minute, I have to go to the bathroom," she said, grabbing her purse.

She knew the way she was twisting her hips was too gaudy, but she wanted to get as many compliments as she could while she had him on his toes. She knew that once he got what he wanted, then the attention would stop just like with all the others. It wasn't fair and she was sick of it.

Elisa went into the bathroom and closed the door. She still didn't feel good about what she planned to do, but knew that if she didn't, Herb would eventually play her like all the rest and leave her with a broken heart and sore pussy.

She didn't like to use her skills to sway the outcome of her relationships, and would rather have everything happen naturally so she could finally have her fairy tale come true. But she was now in her mid-forties and shit wasn't looking good thus far for her love-life. Being lonely was a bitch and that was all she knew for sure.

She looked at herself in the mirror and wondered how she would be able to sleep next to someone who she knew was only there because of her putting some shit in the game. *Well, at least I'll have somebody in my bed,* she reasoned as she dug into her small pocketbook and pulled out a small vial of her homemade love cream. It was kept with her at all times-- just in case. She knew from the countless referrals and repeat customers that the stuff not only worked, but would kick the mythical love potion #9 in the ass.

She smeared a small amount onto the bar of soap that was on the sink, then let the hot water melt it into an undetectable glaze. She left the bar of soap laying in the middle of the sink, making sure she didn't handle it with her bare hands. That would also make Herb think she used the soap after using the restroom. Even if it did look like she was too trifling to put the soap back where she got it, at least she washed her hands.

She went back out into the room to join Herb, still feeling guilty. Instead of dancing, she sat next to him and tried to ease her conscience with a drink. "You gonna let me drink all by myself?" she asked him.

"No, not at all. I was just waiting for you before I opened the other bottle of champagne," he said with a sly grin, as if his player's intuition was letting him know he was about to get down.

Elisa grabbed the bottle and moved to Herb's lap, pouring a big gulp in his mouth for every little sip she took. She knew he would have to pee soon, and hoped he would have the decency to wash his hands afterward.

"Okay, let me up, sweetie," Herb said after twenty minutes of talking and drinking.

Elisa walked over to the window when she heard the door close. She took the champagne to the head like a wino with cottonmouth, trying to drown the guilt inside her.

Elisa pulled off her panties, then unhooked her bra. She laid on the bed with her feet toward the headboard and her head tilted toward the window.

"Mmmm-mmm," Herb said as the former prom queen captured his sight.

Elisa sat up on the edge of the bed, then the backwoods boss of fellatio used her lips and tongue to turn Herb to Stone, trying to give her mixture time to seep into his pores and take effect. "Lay down," she said. She mounted him and stuck her tongue into his mouth, slow-dancing atop his meat. Every time she thought he was about to explode, she would pause and then continue. As she choked his member with her vulva, she softly whispered, "It's the best and it's all yours...forever," into his ear, cultivating his mind with psychological trickery to grow his desire for her while his sexual tangibility was heightened and his judgment was wide open to her suggestions.

* * *

"Why can't I just go in and chill while you dance?" Derek asked Mona.

"'Cause I don't want you in there while I'm workin'. I would feel uncomfortable, then I won't be able to dance like I want to. And if I don't dance right, my money won't be right. So you just gon' have to understand!"

"See, man, I thought we was gon' spend the whole day together," Derek whined.

"Derek, I really had a nice time, but you 'bout to piss me

off. I got to make my money and I don't need you watchin' me while I do it. Damn!"

"Alright then. Call me when you ready to get off."

"Okay. Now let me get in here before my boss be talkin' shit. Here, keep this," Mona said, giving Derek her bracelet. "One of them bitches might break into my locker while I'm on stage." Mona was glad to finally get rid of Derek. He was getting on her nerves and she wanted to go to the birthday party that was going down at the bar that night. She knew all the big ballers would be there, tipping like they had NBA contracts.

She quickly changed, then made her rounds, offering lap dances to anyone who didn't already have an ass in their face.

"I'm straight, but you can give my boy a dance," she heard a voice say from inside the booth. She tried to make out the guy's face, but was blinded by the boogie of his diamond necklace underneath the disco ball. While she danced, she couldn't keep her eyes from wandering to the corner of the booth, to the bling, even though she couldn't make out anything except a fat figure.

"Sit down," the voice said from the corner of the booth.

She slid around into the booth so that she was face to face with the fat guy wearing the ice. "How you doin'?" she asked.

"Naw, how you doin'?" he countered.

"I'm cool. Just tryin' to make a few dollars, that's all."

"That shouldn't be no problem as fine as you is. Can we get together after you get off or somethin'?"

"I don't date customers. Sorry."

"Oh, it's cool. Well, we ain't got to wait till you get off then. What about that?"

"I don't know what you mean."

"I'm just tryin' to help you get a few dollars into yo' pocket like you said you was tryin' to do."

"It sound like you tryin' to get me to ride you right here in this booth."

"What's wrong with that?"

"Not while it's crowded like this. Anybody can be watchin'. I just started workin' here and don't need to lose my job."

"Don't worry about that, my mans own the place. Plus, can't nobody see us with my dogs posted up like they is."

Mona peeped out the scene, and knew she could get away with it, but just didn't like the idea of sexing the fatbody. "Naw, 'cause my man might walk in or somethin'."

"Hold up! Did you say yo' man?"

"Yeah."

"Dig this: my name is Stone, and if you was my woman, I wouldn't hardly let you shake yo' ass in front of no other niggas. He must be broke as hell, 'cause you wouldn't even have to work if you fucked with me."

"No. He take good care of me."

"Not good enough. He gave me a chance to holla at you, and I'm hot. You see, when I get hot like this, I like to wipe my face with about fifteen hun'," he said pulling out an enormous fan of bills to swab his forehead. "So come here and let me get in that thong!"

* * *

Laying in the bed of their elegant hotel room, Johnny and Sonya rested up while watching television. As they talked, Sonya took a soothing breath, realizing that they had never just sat back and kicked it like they were doing. Johnny had even took his time with the sex, giving her foreplay until she was ready for him. The gifts he gave her surprised her. She knew he would spend money on her, but that time he actually gave her things she needed. She felt good, knowing that her patience with him was finally paying off. The thought of the romantic day they were having made her want him again.

"So, did you like your gift?" she asked.

"Man, I like the thought, but the gift was some bullshit! I mean, I don't want you to think I'm ungrateful or nothin', but, Sonya, really, a coupon to get my ass waxed? I ain't that type of nigga. I'm sorry!"

"Aw, baby. You need it, though; your booty is too hairy."

"So I'm just s'posed to lay on the table while somebody put wax on my ass, then take all the hair off? Hell naw!" he laughed, but wasn't kidding.

"I won't tell nobody."

"I know you won't, 'cause it ain't goin' down. Hold up," he said, moving her roaming hand from his leg. "Let me go in the hall and get some more ice."

"Hurry back, or I might cool off." She watched him throw on a robe and make his way out the door. While she waited, she began to imagine having a family with him. Her thoughts were interrupted when she heard a commotion coming from the hallway. *Damn! What the hell is that nigga out there doin'? And I know it's him, too!* she thought as she scrambled to collect her panties and robe.

Sonya made it to the hallway in time to see Johnny holding someone down. The guy's left arm was twisted around Johnny's waist, so he couldn't use his right since Johnny was on his left. As the guy sat on the floor trying to free his arm, Johnny began to slap the shit out of him.

"Nigga, I told you this ain't yo' ice machine," Johnny lectured as he bounced his palm off the guy's face.

Sonya knew Johnny wasn't for games and would likely hurt the guy who looked to be fifteen years older than him. She rushed over and grabbed Johnny. "Stop! Johnny, it's Sweetest Day, baby. Don't mess it up!" Her words seemed to fall on deaf ears as her man continued to spank the face of the helpless man.

"Get off my man!" a female voice shouted as footsteps rapidly approached.

Sonya looked up and nearly fainted. "Auntie!" she began. "Help me get them apart."

"You grab that maniac! It don't look like Herb's doin' too much damage."

After Johnny was finally calmed down, Herb, still out of breath, tried to explain. “I was just tryin' to get us some more ice when this guy came over and start rushin' me.”

“Man, you was takin' all day, and all I did was ask if I could go in front of you 'cause I was in a hurry,”Johnny sparred.

“But, like I said, why can't you just wait like everybody else?”

“Look, I ain't even tryin' to get into all that. Fuck it, take all the ice!”

“That's how it should be! I hate when you young guys try to take over everything like you paid for something,” Herb said, trying to act bad in front of Elisa.

“Man, you better gone on and leave me alone,” Johnny said, trying to count to ten.

Sonya stepped up and grabbed Johnny's arm. “That's right, baby. Come back in the room with me.”

“Ahem!” Elisa said. “Since we all out here, you might as well introduce us.”

“Oh, I'm sorry,” Sonya began. “Johnny, this is my aunt, Elisa, Mona's mother. And, Elisa, this is my boyfriend, Johnny.”

Elisa held out her hand as if she were introducing one of society's elite. “Well, this is my boyfriend, Herb. He's a union steward at one of the auto plants here in Detroit.”

“Oh, okay,” Sonya said, knowing her aunt was trying to be slick, hoping Sonya would tell what Johnny did for a living. “Well, let us get back to our little party.”

After thirty minutes, there was a knock at the door.

“Oh, hi, Herb,” Sonya said as she allowed him to come into their room.

Herb looked to the floor like a scolded youngster made to apologize to neighbors for toilet papering their tree. “Johnny, look, man. I just wanted to apologize for the altercation out there. I had no idea you were part of Elisa's family. If you ever need a job or anything, I'm sure I can get you in at the plant.”

"For real?" Sonya blurted out.

"Oh yeah. I got plenty of pull down there."

"Johnny?" Sonya said, hoping he would jump on the opportunity.

"I'll think about it," Johnny said nonchalantly.

Sonya knew Johnny didn't want or need a job. He made plenty of cash doing what he did best. But she wanted him to get one just to stay out trouble. She hoped that a job might somehow help him become more settled. She knew he would always be the thug at heart she loved so much, but he didn't at all meet her standards as marriage material.

Sonya walked Herb out the door. "He wants the job, he's just a little upset, that's all. I'll talk to him. Thanks a lot, Herb."

Sonya turned slowly after closing the door. She knew she had her work cut out for her. Getting Johnny to do work was like trying to buy a DVD player with food stamps. Sonya met him while he was working at the bar, but what he did there wasn't work. He would just stand around and wait to bounce disorderly people out the door. The auto plant would be hard work, but Sonya figured that once he got in and got used to it, everything would be okay.

One of the main reasons Sonya wanted Johnny to get the job was because she thought that all day while she was at work, he was out screwing other chicks. If he worked, he would be too tired for anybody else and she would have a man who was more faithful. She knew he would cuss her out if she brought it up while he was still pissed about the fight. So before she started her protest, she decided to thaw his icy persona with some heated sexual activity, knowing he wouldn't contest anything said while in her spin-cycle.

Chapter 7

"Let me come in and get your stuff," Herb asked Elisa as they stood in the parking lot of her hotel. "You don't have to stay in no hotel room; you ridin' with Herbie now, baby."

"That's real sweet, but it's too soon for all that. We just met. How can I move in with you already?"

"Us just meeting doesn't matter. It's not like we're in college or nothing. I got a big house, a real nice one, too, but nobody to enjoy it with. I don't want to live alone another day!"

"I can't, Herbie. I already let you talk me out of my panties last night. And by the way, I had a really nice time. Thanks."

"That's what I mean! I had the best time I've had since...I don't even know if I had that much fun before."

"You know just what to say, don't you?"

"Evidently not. You ain't letting me come in and get your things. I want to be with you, making you happy...always."

I knew I used too much cream! Well, I guess this was why I did it in the first place, Elisa thought as she realized Herb was never going to take no for an answer. Knowing he wouldn't care about anything except making her happy, she told him, "Okay then, if you insist. But you better not get me in no drama with no other women you got chasin' you."

"I told you, I ain't got nobody. I'm just a lonely old man who's been waiting for your love to come my way. And since it's here, I'll be damned if I let it get away!"

"Come here," Elisa said, pulling Herb into a delicate kiss. "Now, go get my stuff." As she released him, his eyes sparkled with absent-minded obedience.

"You can just wait out here. Don't worry about a thing; I'll get everything together and bring it out," he said as he opened the door to his caddy for her.

Elisa reclined behind the wheel, waiting for Herb to bring another load of her things to the car. For the first time in years she felt like she had a man. Not just someone she was screwing around with, or had strong feelings for, but her own man. *Oh shit! I forgot about my mixtures!* she thought as she sprang from the caddy to keep Herb from finding the cause of his dreaminess.

She got through the door to find Herb pulling a lotion bottle from onc of her bags. "No don't!" she shouted before he could apply it to his hands. "I'll get this stuff; you can take everything else."

"Let me just get a squirt of that lotion," he asked.

"Boy, this ain't lotion in here. It's a homemade laxative my mom mixed up for me. You don't want none of this," she lied, knowing he was about to saturate his hands with the venom from the spikes of a puffer fish, and could've been reduced to a zombie-like state if just a small amount entered his bloodstream. A teaspoon of the venom could easily kill three adults.

She packed her potions herself, then watched as Herb

gathered the rest of her things.

* * *

After watching her taxi leave, Mona quietly slid her key into the lock, hoping to sneak in without waking Derek.

She felt triumphant knowing that her Kegels had paid off. She did the exercise everyday to keep her pussy tight. She did it so much everyday that it became a habit, and a result of that habit, she turned her trick in the same amount of time that it took for him to roll his rubber on.

Mona never gave in until Stone offered her five hundred for a booth ride. Then, after grabbing the cash, she climbed on his latexed dick and slowly sank her drooling glove while rotating her hips. Before she could reach the base of his shaft, he was motioning for her to get up.

She tried to dodge him the rest of the night, but he kept stalking her, begging her to go home with him where she would receive another five hundred for the night. But she told him, "Look, it costed that much for them fifty seconds you just got. I ain't tryin' to diss you or nothin', but while you was beggin' me to do it, I was gettin' wet and horny. Then, you gon' bust in less than a minute! I'm just kinda pissed about that, 'cause I wanted satisfaction, too; it ain't all about the money," she lied, knowing he was ready to sell his soul for another shot of her refined kitty-cat.

After he upped his offer to the other grand he showed off, she agreed, but told him she wasn't leaving until she finished making her cash at the bar.

At his plush crib, through the course of the night, she allowed him three more times to get down. All three amounted to eight more minutes of sex, which gave her fifteen hundred, plus five hundred more from the bar. So, she didn't give a damn what Derek had to say because she had Stone's nose open like a casino on the Vegas strip. She could tell from the paraphernalia Stone failed to put away that he dealt heroin. And she was a vet when it came to that thanks to her late ex., and also her late father who used her for a lookout when she was eleven back in the projects when he pushed black tar.

Mona looked around as she dropped her jacket and purse. No Derek. She crept up the stairs. There was Derek, shaking his head with a disgusted look on his face.

"That's how it's gon' be, huh?"

She twisted her face as if she did nothing wrong. "What you talkin' 'bout?"

"I'm talkin' 'bout you comin' up in here at eight in the mornin'."

"I know you ain't trippin' when you ain't even ask me why."

"Okay, why?"

"I went to the casino with my girl from the bar."

"Yeah, right!"

"Nigga, I ain't got to lie to you!"

"What was her name then?"

"Goldie. You might know her."

"I think you been out fuckin' 'round all night!"

"See, that's why I don't like to fuck wit' niggas I meet at the bar. I was at the casino! We ain't know what time it was; ain't no windows or clocks in there. Shit, I was ridin' with her, so I couldn't just leave while she was tryin' to win her money back."

"I bet you lost all the money you made last night, didn't you?"

"Hell naw! I won five hundred," she smiled, trying to sedate him with a portion of her dough. "You want it? You can have it if you think I'm lyin'. You know I ain't just gon' give you no money I had to shake my ass for, either."

"Naw, that's alright. I'm cool," he said, seeming to cool down a bit.

"Hold up, I just thought of somethin'. You just think I'm a ho, don't you?"

"Why you say that?" he asked, looking as if he were about to fold under her witty offense.

"You accusin' me of fuckin' all night. You should know I ain't into trickin' from our fallin' out yesterday. Now you gon' accuse me of fuckin'? I was happy from doin' good at the casino, ready to lace you up with some head for bein' so understandin', but I think this is yo' way of lettin' me know I would be wrong to go against my own beliefs and make you happy. 'Cause you can forget that shit now! Matter of fact, you ain't even gettin' none of this pussy, either. I'll show you how easy I am!" she asserted, trying to reserve her sex as much as possible for her flesh game. She had turned tricks before back home when she used to strip, until her ex got her out of that life and allowed her to help prepare the dope he sold.

"Man, you on some bullshit," Derek said. "I think I'll hang at the casino tonight; I feel kinda lucky myself."

"Go ahead. Be my guest. But don't expect me to stay in this big house by myself all night; it's too scary."

"What? You just tryin' to stay out again."

"No I ain't. But I'll leave if you ain't gon' be here with me. Look, I'm tired of arguin'. You want somethin' to eat before I lay down?"

"Yeah, hook me up."

"I got you. My mother taught me how to make some bomb-ass spaghetti."

"Cool!"

"Oh yeah, I almost forgot to tell you 'bout my girl with the little hook-up."

"What kind of hook-up?"

"She was sayin' somethin' 'bout some dope, but I told her I really didn't know about it."

"You what? What she say? Did she give you some prices?"

"Oh, you sell dope?" she quizzed, having had some idea that he was a hustler.

"How you think I make all my money? Shit, I could use a new plug, too. See what she talkin' 'bout and let me know. I can sell just about anything."

"I don't like bein' in the middle of that junk."

"C'mon, baby. Don't you wanna see yo' man come up?"

"You know I do," she purred. "I know she was sayin' somethin' about some dog food. You know what that mean?"

"Yeah. What she say?"

"I think her man sell it. But, he'll let her get it real cheap so she can make a few dollars. She'll probably give me some real cheap if I want it, but I don't know cause you fuss at me too much and that ain't cool!"

"Aw, baby, you know I was just horny. Come in here with me so I can make it up to you."

"No. I told you, you ain't gettin' none."

"I know you did, but that was before you knew I was gon' blow up off that new plug," he said. His eyes gleamed as if he already had the dope.

Mona was excited herself thinking of the way Derek jumped on the bait. She gave in to Derek's lust and hoped he would be a damned good hustler, knowing she would have no problem getting dope out of Stone once he slipped up and mentioned it to her.

* * *

"So how did it go with Gwen?" Johnny asked Ross. The two of them sat in Johnny's living room sipping gin and watching videos.

"Man, c'mon, you know me. She gave me a little resistance, but we got down. And once she opened up, I had a tiger on my hands."

"Straight up?"

"Yeah. I like her, man."

"It's like that?"

"Yeah. She good people. She ain't fulla bullshit like all these bitches in the 'hood. She liked the purses, but I can tell she ain't really material like that."

"That's good, 'cause from what I hear, li'l cuz might have his hands full with Mona."

"She out there, huh?"

"Aw, man! Sonya's friend said she saw her ridin' a nigga in a booth at the bar."

"Tricked out!"

"Got to be! She called Sonya just when I was 'bout to roll over on her ass. It's a good thing her and Sonya be actin' like they don't know each other at work. She must know she off the hook. You know, it really wouldn't surprise me if Derek wound up marryin' a broad like that; them the types of headaches he fuck wit'."

"Damn. So, whatever happened with that situation between him and Smurf?"

"I ain't heard nothin, but I'm willin' to bet he's still in that nigga's pocket."

"So what you wanna do about it?"

"I'm tryin' to wait till Smurf get ready to get on again. I know Derek gon' ask me for the loot to cover his bill again when Smurf get ready to re-up."

"You think that's when Derek's money is due?"

"That's what I'm hopin'."

"So, we can get him for his re-up dough when we do him."

"Right! And I know that nigga get at least five or six hundred of them thangs."

"Cool! What time we gon' holla at the cable man?"

"It's 'bout that time; might as well ride. Oh yeah, I forgot to tell you about Mona's mother's boyfriend comin' back to the room to apologize."

"And he got his ass whupped?"

"Yeah. But dig, he told me he can get me a job at the plant he work at if I want."

"Straight up?"

"Yeah. I ain't tryin' to fuck with that shit."

"Man, are you crazy? That's good money, plus you get benefits, and it's all kinds of other hook-ups you can get working there. You how many niggas get a job there, then go out on medicals forever?"

"Damn, I ain't never look at it like that," Johnny said as they hopped into Ross's van.

"Tell ol' boy I'll give him a gee to get me in."

At Ross's house, Benny pulled up in his cable van. He was the master of bootleg cable. He had a young neighbor, Ramone, who sold ecstasy pills across the alley from where Benny lived. Having a white woman who wasn't from the 'hood, and was terrified to have a drug house behind her residence, Benny tried to talk the young hustler out of his pill-game. But everybody knows that when you got a spot doing more than a grand a day, you keep it rollin'. And after the police raid, you crank it right back up. There was no reasoning with the young cat, so Benny hired Johnny to try to scare him away.

After pulling the van into Benny's backyard, Johnny and Ross hopped out and went over the back fence into Ramone's yard. They kicked in the side door, then scrambled to subdue Ramone. Once they had him in the kitchen ready to be tied up, his woman jumped out of the broom closet, swinging a butcher knife like she had on a ski mask. Johnny side-stepped her attack and the knife stuck into the wall. Seized from behind, she lay breathless underneath Johnny after collapsing under his weight. Her hands were then tied behind her back.

Johnny looked back at Ross who was struggling with the young thug. Being twice Ross's size, the young thug nearly threw Ross on his ass before Johnny slammed his knuckles into Ramone's rib cage, knocking the wind out of him. Once he collapsed, Ross grabbed him in a full nelson while Johnny went back to work on his body.

Johnny basted Ramone in the gut until the young thug puked, then told Ross to stand him up so he could beat him some more.

"What the fuck do y'all want?" Ramone strained to ask.

"Oh, damn. I guess we forgot to tell you about that," Ross

joked. "You got to get the fuck on wit' them X's; niggas don't want that bullshit 'round here."

Johnny got back to work on Ramone's body, shooting underhanded torpedoes at his gut until Ramone went limp.

"Stop! Y'all muthafuckas gon' kill him!" Ramone's woman screamed.

"What? You gon' talk to him for us so we don't have to come back?" Johnny asked.

"Yeah! I'll do it! I'll make sure he don't sell dope no more. Just don't hurt us or our baby!"

"Okay," Johnny began. "'Cause if I have to come back, it's gon' be a gravedigger gettin' paid to handle this nigga's stankin' ass!" Johnny hit Ramone a few more times and caused him to wake and dry-heave.

"Damn, Ross, that nigga almost got down on you," Johnny joked as they left.

"Right. You know that young punk probly ain't never puffed a square or nothin', just healthy as a ox."

"You better start doin' cardio exercises if you gon' be smokin' all them blunts, nigga!"

Chapter 8

On the eve of Thanksgiving, Johnny and Ross watched T.V. with Herb while their ladies labored in the kitchen. The ladies cleaned chitlins, and Herb proved to be an annoying suck-ass, saying anything he could think of to fit in. Ross gave Johnny the eye. The *damn, I hope this nigga shut up* eye.

Why the fuck do this nigga talk so damned much? Johnny thought. "Hey, Ross, why don't you ride with me to get some more drinks?" Johnny said, trying to escape the babbling extrovert.

"Oh, y'all going to the store?" Herb asked. "I'll go. You two are pretty cool to hang out with."

"Y'all go ahead," Ross declined. "I'm gon' stay here and make sure the girls are safe."

Johnny looked to Ross and squinted, reflecting his aggravation. *I see you laughin', nigga! I'm gon' fix yo' ass!*

Even though Herb opted to pay for everything, Johnny was still pissed about being around him, so he stabbed Sonya's small Honda toward the apartment. When they parked the car, they were shocked to see Sonya and Elisa running out to Elisa's car.

"Where y'all goin'?" asked Johnny.

Sonya ran up breathing hard. "Look, baby, you gotta lay low!"

"What?" Johnny said as his mouth instantly went dry. He stepped out into the cool dusk air to keep Herb from hearing whatever she had to say.

"The police were here lookin' for you. You gotta get outta here! Take Ross's van. Now! Before they come back!"

"Where the fuck is Ross?"

"They took him. Some homicide detectives. They took Gwen too 'cause she jumped in and started fightin' when they was tryin' to cuff him. Please, please, Johnny, go! Please, baby, go. Don't let 'em get you," she begged with her fingers interlocked under her chin as if she were praying.

"I don't got the keys to his van."

Elisa threw the keys, then hopped into her Cadillac. "C'mon, Sonya! We gotta at least get Gwen."

"Bye, baby. Please go! I'll find you...you know I will, but don't come around here right now!"

Johnny left Herb in Sonya's car as he hopped into the van. His heart tried to leap out of his chest as he stabbed out of the complex. *Damn, I'm glad he kept this van in the broker's name,* he thought, knowing he might have to sleep in the RV until he could find out what was going on.

He knew if he were to come back to the apartment, a homicide stake-out would be waiting to snare him. With all the dirt he and his homeboy had done, he had no idea which job the police wanted him for, but he knew Ross would never give any info.

Hating to have to sleep in the van, Johnny thought about his weekend girl. "Hello, Angelique? It's me, Johnny!"

"What the hell you callin' me for? You ain't called in a

month! I don't want to talk to yo' ass now!" <Click!>

Bitch! At least I got a TV in here. Damn, Gwen is a soldier for real. Jumped on them bitches for tryin' to take her man. That's what I'm talkin' 'bout! At least I got away from Herb's irksome ass!

* * *

It was only eight-o-clock and Mona was already capitalizing on the holiday crowd at the bar, coercing the soft to not only pay for a dance, but to buy her a drink as well. She could feel Stone's high-beams burning holes in her ass as she strutted around the bar looking for a come-up.

Her little business venture was finally paying off with him. In one of his flamboyant moments, he tried to dazzle her by boasting about the hold he had on the heroin game in the city.

"Oh, yeah? You the man, huh, baby?" she drawled as she climbed into his plethoric bed to straddle him and lubricate his dick with her vaginal truth serum.

"Man, hell yeah! Shit, it's gettin' to the point that I might have to hire somebody else to help me hook my shit up. I got too much goin' on now. I can't spread myself that thin. Oohhh-aahh!" he moaned as she began her sexual sorcery.

"Why you ain't ask me to help you? I know how to get down. And you know I got yo' back, baby."

"What you know 'bout that boy?" he asked as his eyelids veiled his pupils.

"C'mon now! I can serve it up hard or soft." She planted a sugary kiss on Stone's lips.

"Might as well, you fine mu'fucka, you!"

"I got you!" she said, cutting her convo short so Stone could succumb to her suction pussy.

The next day she proved her words true as she broke down a mushroom of dope, then mixed it. She passed on the use of the small spoon Stone tried to hand her for measuring, and instead used the corner of a playing card, making thirty-two perfect dime-blows from a gram for Stone's moneyspot. She then amazed him by wrapping the leftover dope in plastic, and using the holes in the center of a ceramic brick as molds, she pressed it hard again by rolling a car tire over it. She made perfect quarter-ounce sized Cuban fingers. Since he used a machine, she knew the re-rock method would surely gain his vote. Knowing she could slang grams for a hundred-fifty, she used her female influence to Jew his price down to sixty dollars a gram for her. Since that day, three weeks ago, she used Derek to flip nearly a quarter-kilo.

She knew Stone had been curious about who she was doing business with and would keep watching her. She also noticed a short guy staring like he wanted to spend with her. She went right over to him. “Can I help you?” she asked.

“What you mean?” asked the short guy.

“You been starin' at me all night.”

“I can't look? You the finest thang in here.”

“Well, since I'm over here, you might as well buy me a drink and get a dance.”

In their booth, Mona began her first-impression groove, grinding and gyrating as seductively as she possibly could. “What's your name?”

“Smurf.”

“That's cute.” *Oh shit! Is that Johnny? What's he doin' here? Sonya don't even work today*, she thought while trying to turn out of Johnny's view.

Johnny looked around until he scoped her out, then came right over.

“What's up, Johnny?” Smurf said. “Sit down.”

“What's goin' on?” Johnny asked, pretending to not know Mona.

“I'm glad I saw you, man. You know your cousin been dodgin' me.”

“Who, Derek?”

“Yeah. He owe me a lot of money. I hope me and you can come together to straighten that shit out, man.”

"I don't got nothin' to do with that, dude. That's all cuz."

"Okay," Smurf said in a way that let Mona know that Derek was out there bad.

"Yeah, man. My mans Ross got swooped by the hook. They took his woman, too, so I got to deal with that."

Oh shit! Mona thought, knowing Gwen had never experienced the murky cruelties of the lockup.

After her dance, Mona went to her locker to check her voicemail messages. Her mailbox was overflowing with calls from Sonya and her mother. She quickly changed and left the bar, catching Johnny just as he was pulling out of the parking lot. "I'm glad I caught you," she said to Johnny.

"You talk to Sonya or anybody?"

"Naw, I just got my messages."

"Gwen should be cool. Hopefully they only hit her with resisting and obstructing. Just a misdemeanor."

"That girl ain't never been in no jail or nothin'."

"Sonya said she tried to jump on the police for tryin' to arrest Ross."

"That's Gwen alright. She quiet, but make her mad and she'll be at that ass."

"I see! She ain't wanna see them niggas take her man."

"That's 'cause she know how foul them police do people back home. They probably ain't like that here. What did they arrest Ross for?"

"Sonya said they was homicide detectives, so..."

"Ooohhh. I can't picture him hurtin' nobody."

"Can you picture me hurtin' somebody, 'cause they lookin' for me, too!"

"Shit! What you gon' do?"

"I damn sho' ain't turnin' myself in! They just gon' have to catch me."

"So you can't even go home?"

"That's right, 'cause you know the dickheads will be posted up, waitin' for a nigga."

"Can you take me home? I ain't wanna have Derek comin' up here and that man in there talkin' like he wanna do somethin' to him."

"He did seem kind of pissed, didn't he?"

"That was smooth the way you played it off, too."

"I know everything ain't right with me so ain't no use gettin' everybody else hot, too. Just tell Derek what you heard so he can be cool. But, he got to already know Smurf lookin' for his ass."

"You gon' just let that nigga do somethin' to your family like that?"

"It ain't really a whole lot I can do right now; I'm hot as a box cutter in a airport. I just fell through so you can know what was up with yo' peeps."

As they rode towards Mona's, she wondered how Derek could owe someone with all the cash he was making from the dope she was giving him. *What the hell is he doing with his money? He better not be spending it on some other chick!*

* * *

Charges against Gwen were dropped the same night since the detectives were so happy to have Ross in custody. Johnny took Sonya and Gwen to the grocery store for last minute items while he picked Gwen's brains for details involving the warrants.

Johnny listened intently while reclining in the driver seat to keep out of the view of any squad cars.

"Yeah, so they were saying something about a cableman got arrested and told who did the murders," Gwen said.

"Who got murdered?"

"They said a woman and her baby who lived across the alley from the cableman."

"What?" Johnny shouted. "That nigga lyin' if he said we killed that ho! She was alive when we left!"

"Oh, so y'all did go over there?" Gwen asked.

"We went by there, but I'm tellin' you, we ain't kill nobody.

We didn't even get to see that baby. Did they say anything 'bout the nigga that live there?" Johnny asked.

"He was handcuffed and shot, but tried to play dead so he wouldn't get killed, too."

"And the cableman said we did it?"

"Yup!"

As they parked at the grocery store, Johnny saw Benny's van in the parking lot. Then, saw Benny walking out of the store with his old lady. "That's that lyin'-ass cableman right there!" Johnny shouted, sliding into his parking space.

"Where?" asked Gwen as she scanned the parking lot. "That dude with the bags, walking with that lady?"

"Yeah," Johnny said. Before he could make a move to go after Benny, Gwen had her coat off and was out the door. "Where you goin'?"

"That punk got my man locked up," Gwen said.

"Hold up, girl. Wait for me!" Sonya said as she hopped out and ran behind Gwen.

Johnny couldn't believe his eyes and ears. He grabbed his bottle of bumpy-face and took it to the head. He got down low so that only his eyes were above the dashboard as he watched the ladies rush over like hunting lionesses out to vanquish and devour Benny.

Benny's woman got behind him, but he began backing up as Gwen and Sonya closed in with aimed index fingers and fast-moving lips, obviously checking him. Then, as Johnny took another swallow, it happened. Benny's woman ran for cover as Sonya circled around behind and shoved him toward Gwen. Gwen swung and tagged Benny in the jaw. Benny's bags fell to the ground.

Being no slouch in the stick-and-move department, Sonya stepped in and started drilling Benny in the face with pugilistic accuracy. As he used his arms to guard his grill, a crowd formed around the squabble.

Somehow Gwen got Benny's coat over his head while

Sonya continued her relentless jabs. Gwen then lifted two cans of corn and began beating Benny in the back with them.

Benny's girl stood in the crowd and watched the whole thing with the security guard who seemed to be more interested in his own entertainment than Benny's safety.

Knowing the police would soon show up, Johnny hopped out and ran to retrieve the vicious women.

Hell yeah! I got a soldier, too! he thought as he cheesed with child-like enthusiasm. He took Sonya to a low-key motel room on Telegraph and rewarded her for making him so proud by laying some tongue-fu on her for the first time.

Chapter 9

Mona saw the fear in Derek when she told him about Smurf's convo with Johnny. She knew Derek wasn't the type to carry guns, and probably wouldn't know what to do with one if he had one. She wanted to go out shopping, but Derek was too shook to leave the house.

"Derek, I want to go to the mall."

"I don't feel like doin' nothin' right now. Maybe later," he said.

"Just let me use your car," she said, knowing the real reason he wasn't going. Thinking of the way he probably felt made her feel sorry for him. She also felt guilty for allowing him to jack-off his money on her when he could've been using it to pay his ticket. Then her mind flashed back to the thoughts of the cash he was making from the dope she was giving him. "Derek, can I ask you somethin'? How can you owe a nigga enough for him to wanna do somethin' to you when you makin' a lot of money from the stuff I get for you?"

"Man, I don't really want to talk about that with you."

"What you mean, you don't want to talk about it with me?

Who do you talk about it with?"

"What? I don't talk about money with nobody."

"Well, you better not be spendin' yo' shit on some other bitch, 'cause if you is, you can just have her bring you dope and shit!"

"Man, cut it out! I ain't got nobody but you."

"Then what you doin' with all yo' money, Derek?" she asked, her face displaying concern.

"I told you, I would rather not kick it with you about that."

"Okay then, since I ain't good enough to kick it with about some serious shit like that, then you get whoever you kick it with to run your drugs to you. 'Cause I told you, I don't like bein' in the middle of that shit anyway. I just do it to help you out, and I ain't good enough to talk to!" she said, guilt-tripping him to death. She snatched up the car keys and headed toward the door. She knew if nothing else got to Derek it would be the loss of the dope plug.

"Damn, man! Look, I ain't got no other chicks! It's bad out in the streets right now. Niggas is robbin' and shit. They just ain't playin' the game right no more."

Sitting down, she listened to him begin to open up to her.

"I got robbed twice since I got that plug with your girl. I just made up the loss out my own pocket to keep her dealin' with me."

"Who robbed you?"

"It don't even matter. I'm straight now, but my pockets just ain't like they should be 'cause niggas out here so shady. I got a few true hustlers that I'm workin' with now, but I still ain't really makin' the money I should be makin' 'cause I got to go so low with my prices to keep my few customers 'cause they rather go to they other people that they came up with to get their dope. I can work the heroin, but it's not my regular bag, so I got to scrape together all new clientèle and it's trial and error findin' out who's straight and who's scurvy. This shit here ain't like sellin' weed."

"Derek, if you ain't makin' yo' money, I don't think it's really worth the risk."

"I know it will be worth it if I stick with it. It's just slow startin' out for me."

Well strap on yo' nuts and get busy, baby, she thought as she got up to leave again. "I'm sorry I pried into your business like that, I just..."

"I know. Go ahead to the mall. I'll see you when you get back."

Whipping Derek's Ford Explorer down Greenfield, Mona saw that she was riding on fumes. She pulled into the gas station at the corner of Seven mile.

As she walked to the window to pay for the gas, a hateful wind nearly blew her over. She could hear a group of guys laughing inside a Caprice Classic. As she started back toward the truck, the Caprice's door opened and out poured a cloud of bud smoke and a dark-skinned joker with his pants sagging damn-near to his knees.

"Hey, baby. Let me holla at you for a minute."

"You gon' pump my gas?" she asked.

"If that's the only way I can talk to you," he said.

"Well, I got ten dollars on pump six." She stood next to the truck as the guy pumped the gas. "So what's goin' on? You better talk if you got somethin' to say, 'cause I'm on my way somewhere."

The guy looked like he couldn't believe he had a chance to kick it with her. "Well, dig, I'm Roy Jr. I was just checkin' you out and was wonderin' if we could exchange numbers or somethin'.

"You can give me yours."

"Aw, so you don't really wanna holla at a nigga, do you? Just keep it real. I understand. I see how fine you are, and I know you probably married or somethin'."

Mona tried to watch the traffic going down the street to keep from looking at the guy's face. She didn't want to laugh, thinking that he looked like a sea-donkey. He was just that ugly to her. But she could tell he was thugged-out to the max! The type of nigga who wouldn't hesitate to do dirt, and she knew she just might need someone like that in her very near future.

She knew that if she would've noticed he and his crew before, she would've been leery of being robbed. They looked to be the type of niggas who would all share the same forty-ounce; scavengers, fresh out the alley.

Figuring he might somehow prove useful, she decided to snatch him up. "I just moved up here from down South, so I'm stayin' with some family right now and I don't want to be givin' they number out like that. That's why I said, 'you can give me your number. I'll call you, I ain't married."

"Straight up?" he asked in awe.

She looked shocked, not expecting him to reveal his excitement over the green light she gave.

"I mean, cool," he said, trying to keep secret how geeked up he was. "I know niggas been at you since you got here, huh?"

Mona just blushed, playing along.

"I know. Well, here's my digits. I gotta get back to my ride before one of them niggas steal some of my CD's," he said, scribbling his number. He backed away watching her.

Knowing he was still scoping her out, Mona deliberately rolled her hips, advertising her ass in an attempt to boost his fascination. Opening the door, she looked at him in time to see his smile ignite as one of his boys shouted, "Yeah, nigga!"

She could tell by the way he was on her that he would be easily manipulated, and she knew she had it going on. Her strip thang, and her dope thang, and could serve it up hard or soft. And that's just what she planned to do, serve up the niggas; the hard and the soft.

* * *

Elisa walked hand-in-hand with Herb through the lobby of a movie theater in Southfield. He had been calling her on every one of his breaks everyday while at work. At first, the attention he was showing her was wonderful, but now he was becoming a nuisance. He would do all the cooking and cleaning, would paint her toenails, and even wash the clothes.

She knew he only meant good and was only trying his best to please her, but she did like some private time to think, and just breath. She liked going out, too, but doing it every day was taking the thrill out of it.

Herb got in line for snacks while Elisa went into the restroom. While coming out, she bumped into an older woman.

"Mrs. Benoit, how are you?" the woman said like an excited devotee.

Elisa looked over to the refreshment counter hoping that Herb was too busy to notice. But, he was headed her way. She didn't recognize the woman, but knew since she had never visited Detroit the woman could've only known her from back home. "Hello," Elisa said in a low tone, hoping the woman would catch on and lower her voice.

"I know you may not remember me, but I once visited you with my cousin, Stacey Brooks."

"Oh yeah. The woman whose son was mauled by her neighbor's dog. I vaguely remember your face, but just couldn't place you. How are things with your cousin?"

"Well, she's fine, but now I'm having trouble."

Elisa looked up to see Herb in ear's range, coming with popcorn and drinks. "Just take down my number and give me a call later," Elisa speed-talked, trying to shake the woman before Herb got wise.

"Okay, but here." The woman reached into her purse and pulled out a polaroid of a slender black man dressed like a pimp. "This is my problem. He has my daughter strung-out on drugs, and makes her sell her precious ass in the streets. Please help me, Mrs. Benoit! Do something to bring my baby back home."

Elisa took the picture, then turned to see Herb's reaction. He was alert as a deer, but her cover wasn't blown yet. Elisa gave the woman her number after tucking the photograph. “I'll be waiting for your call.”

“Oh, thank you! Thank you! It's such a blessing for me to see you here in Detroit. Here, I'll give you the guy's address.”

“Don't worry about it, I have all I need,” Elisa said, knowing she could whack the pimp with as little as a photo, a few strands of hair, or even one of his dirty socks. “Call me tonight when you have your daughter with you. I have to go, our show is about to start,” she said seeing that the woman would've kept talking and carrying on until Herb knew everything.

“What was that all about?” Herb asked with a confused look.

“Oh, just someone from back home. She was just happy to see me, that's all.”

“No, she acted like you were some kind of celebrity or something.”

“People are just different back home than they are here. Are we going to see the movie or what?”

“Oh, yeah. It's almost time.” Herb still had a puzzled look on his face as they walked to their seats.

Elisa wondered how she was going to handle her biz with Herb up in her grill all the time.

Later that evening, Elisa's phone rang. “Hello,” she answered. It was the woman and she had her daughter at home with her, but told Elisa she had to hurry because her daughter would soon be fiendin' for another hit of dope.

Deciding to take Herb's car in case he tried to follow, Elisa told him, “I'm going to meet my friend from the theater for a drink.”

“Well we could have a drink together if you just want a drink.”

“That's not it, Herb. We're just going to have a little girl talk. We haven't seen one another for some time and just want to catch up on things.”

"Okay, I just don't want you to feel like you have to go somewhere else for something I could've been doing with you."

Elisa stood over Herb in his chair and kissed his bald head. "You're doing just fine, baby."

Elisa arrived at the woman's house after twenty minutes and sat the woman's daughter down, counseling her. She told her how the man in her life was only her downfall, and that she would do much better without him, trying to make her see for herself why she was in the situation she was in. After thirty minutes of talking, Elisa saw that the young woman was beginning to see things clearly. "I want you to write your boyfriend's name on this piece of paper," she told her. Elisa then walked the young woman to the kitchen stove. "Now take that piece of paper and burn it," Elisa instructed, knowing that part of her solution was purely psychological. "Now what you must do is help yourself by choosing your friends better, young lady. You can do so much better than that guy who obviously doesn't care about you."

After receiving her cash, Elisa went back home to Herb, knowing she would have to do her part with the polaroid later that night when he was asleep.

* * *

Johnny wrote down every number in his cellphone, then cruised across the Belle Isle bridge, hurling the phone into the Detroit river. He had realized that his phone had GPS capabilities, and figured the authorities could possibly track him down just as they do with the units in the luxury cars. He had already purchased another less expensive phone under an alias name where he put all of his important contact numbers.

He had received word that Toya, a stripper at the Triangle, was trying to contact him. Johnny knew she was a solid chick, one who could handle most beefs herself, so he knew if she wanted his help, it had to be something deep.

"Yo, Toya," he said into his phone. "Meet me in the parking

lot on Southfield and Outer Drive. I'll see your car."

After a thirty minute wait, he saw her coming out of a bookstore in the strip mall wearing dark shades. He followed her to her car, then parked next to it. He watched as she sat in her car, unbuttoning the top two buttons on her blouse, fluffing her tits as if she had a discount in mind.

"Hey, what's up, Toya?" he asked as she hopped into the passenger seat with a somber look.

"Hey."

"So, what's the deal with you?"

"Man, you ain't gon' believe this shit." She slowly removed her shades and shook her head, revealing her face. Her eye looked like it was lodged inside a volcano, red with a swollen black ring around it.

Johnny jumped at the sight. "Damn! Who the hell did that?"

"My sister's baby daddy. That nigga just got out of jail and came by. He was always cool with the family, so I let him in."

"What's his name?"

"Marlon."

"Marlon?" Johnny asked in amazement.

"Yeah, you know him?"

"Where did he live before he went to the joint?"

"Over on Clements with some chick."

"They let that ho-ass nigga out?"

"Yeah. But let me tell you what happened. Like I said, he was always tight with the family, playing with the kids and shit. So I let him in, and we talked for about thirty minutes, then he asked about my son. I told him to go to the back room where my son was playing, right? Now I'm up front talkin' on the phone to my girlfriend and I hear my son screamin' and shit, so I runs back there to find this grown-ass mu'fucka holdin' my son down, sittin' on his chest suckin' his dick!"

"What?!"

"I bullshit you not!"

"I knew that nigga used to smoke and shit, but I ain't know

he was out his mind like that!"

"Listen! I kicked him in his back, tryin' to get him up off my baby, right? That nigga got up and busted me in my shit, then snatched my jewelry off my neck. Look at my neck." She turned toward Johnny, showing two red scrapes across her collarbone, the evidence of Marlon's vicious thievery.

"Johnny, if you see how big that nigga got, you might be able to imagine how much pain I was in. But right then, I was really too mad to feel it. I was only worried about my son. My punk-ass brothers was actin' like they was scared of him and shit 'cause he so big now.

"I mean, I don't give a fuck about the jewelry, I just want that nigga dead! I heard from somebody that was locked up in there with him that he was in there fuckin' wit' them sissies, but you know how rumors are. I gives this nigga the benefit of the doubt and now I got to pay you to kill him."

"You know what I charge, right?" Johnny asked, remembering her tit fluffs before she got in.

"Yeah. Ol' boy who gave me your number already told me, and I got that right now." She reached into her Salvatore Ferragamo handbag and whipped out a pregnant envelope. After handing him the envelope, she asked, "You mind if I check out your van? I was thinkin' 'bout gettin' one."

"I don't care," he said, flipping through the scrill, counting with bank teller swiftness. By the time he got to the end of the bills, he looked to see what Toya was doing. His eyes bucked and his dick bloated with sexual want.

"Come back here," she said, reclining in one of the rear seats with her skirt hiked above her wide hips and Ferragamo heels pointing to the ceiling. "I got a little bonus for you, just to make sure you put Marlon at the top of your priority list."

It's a good thing she put them shades back on. I told myself I wasn't gon' cheat on Sonya no more, but this bitch thick as hell! Johnny thought as he snatched a ribbed, super-sensitive condom from the glove compartment. He then beat down her hairy snatch like he was a fresh parolee and she was a fine-ass basehead, six dollars short on happiness.

Chapter 10

Ross sat on the old side of the Wayne County Jail, pissed, thinking of all the cash in the streets he was missing. He couldn't wait to see Gwen again. Her visits were the good in his life that kept him in a sound mood and out of trouble. Since the death of her hooptie, she would drive Ross's Impala and stay as long as she could.

Ross was no stranger to the system, and knew it was a blessing to have a woman like Gwen in his corner. She'd just gotten a job as a billing specialist and was holding down his crib, taking care of all his business. He at first didn't know if he could trust her with his things, his every things, but he knew he would be a lot better off if he did gamble on her.

Now, it was paying off and she was his everything. She had many rare, old-fashioned qualities that set her far apart from most of the women in Detroit. But to Ross, her devotion to her man made her shine the most.

Whenever the coast was clear, Ross would tell Gwen, "Ain't nobody around. Pop 'em out." She would pull up her shirt and flash her titties. She kept his account fat, and even paid to have a few joints slipped in to him.

He was sick knowing he was in the cage for something he didn't do, but began to realize that he wasn't there for the instant offense, but because of something he had maybe done some other time. That's the way he believed the universal law worked.

To make matters worse, Johnny was on the run and couldn't help much since communicating with him was so difficult. Ross did manage to let him know through Gwen that the dead woman's insurance company was investigating the murder. That was the one thing that gave him some relief, knowing that the insurance company would dig deeper into the facts and find out what really went down, just in case they could get out of cashing out on the policy.

If it was left up to the Detroit Police, he knew he would've been doing a life bit, 'cause they don't care about what really went on, they just want to close murder cases.

"You doin' alright?" Ross asked Gwen.

"Yeah, I'm okay. I just miss you, that's all."

"I miss you, too," he said, placing his palm on the glass where her hand was.

"I been praying for you, and I know you'll be out soon."

"I hope so, but right now, it ain't lookin' so good."

"Why you say that."

"One of the victims was a baby, so it would take some solid evidence to get a nigga out of some shit like that. Even if they know they got the wrong person, his ass is still locked down 'cause they can't allow society to think that a baby-killer is on the loose."

"Whatever happens, I'll be right by your side," she said with so much sincerity that her eyes flooded with tears. Her words were so powerful that they stimulated Ross mentally, filling the void of his heart.

"Damn!" he said, thinking of being separated from something so precious. "I wish I woulda met you a long time ago. Not while I'm goin' through this bullshit. I think we was 'bout to have some really special shit between us. I mean, I can feel the vibes that you give off, like you was created just for me."

"I do, too; that's why I'm here. And I'll still be here when you get out. My friends will too." She raised her shirt and exposed the twins.

* * *

Johnny chilled in the van in the parking lot of the apartments where Marlon was said to live. He had been staking the place out for three days and still no Marlon. Only a woman dressed like a hooker.

She lived alone, but would have male company every night, usually a white guy.

Johnny knew Marlon hated him for taking Angelique, Marlon's old girlfriend, so the thought of killing Marlon made him feel better anyway. He couldn't imagine life having to look over his shoulder.

Having the feeling that he'd been given the wrong info, he called Toya. "Hello? This Johnny. No, not yet. I'm at the address, but I don't think he live here. Don't nobody go in or out 'ccpt some woman."

"Well, that's where my sister said he lives," she said.

"Somebody told her wrong 'cause ain't nobody there 'cept some broad. I'll keep you posted, though."

Johnny decided to swing by Benny's to finish him for ratting them out. On the way, Johnny saw one of the neighborhood dopefiends, Count Basie, who used to run with Marlon.

Johnny whipped around the block to allow Basie time to go into the store so he couldn't see what Johnny was driving. After parking, Johnny hopped out and went into the store.

Basie was inside wearing a funky-looking hoody. The

drawstring for the hood was tight around his face and fashioned into a bow under his chin. He was trying to buy a two-dollar beer with eighty cents.

"What's up, Johnny?" Basie asked. "Loan me a dollar."

Johnny handed him a dollar, hoping he might give some info on Marlon. "What's been up with you?"

"Nothin' much," Basie said. "Just stayin' below the radar. Tryin' to keep out of trouble."

"You ain't hollered at yo' boy, Marlon?"

"You mean Marla?"

"Why you say that?" Johnny asked, pretending to know nothing of Marlon's new sexual preference.

"Man, that nigga is a stone fag! Somebody was tamperin' wit' that ass when he was locked up, 'cause he out here bad! Dressin' up like a broad, sellin' them buns on Woodward and Six mile."

"You say they tamperd with 'em, huh?" Johnny asked with a laugh.

"Yeah. Somebody definitely got a hold of 'em, 'cause he went in bitchin' and came out switchin'."

Dressin' up like a lady? Johnny thought as the truth struck him. "You say he be trickin' where?"

"Woodward and Six. And if you thinkin' 'bout trickin' wit' him, you might be outta luck, 'cause he only deal with white boys."

Johnny's face wrinkled at the Count's wise crack. "Nigga--"

"I'm just bullshittin' wit' you," the Count said while easing his way out the door, slipping a meat stick up his sleeve.

Johnny cruised Woodward all night, looking for Marlon. The whole set looked like a circus. The thing that shocked Johnny the most was the amount of whites that were in the area trying to pick up gays.

Johnny knew that finding Marlon amongst the queers was like finding a needle in a pile of needles.

Johnny went into a store on Six mile and bought a six-pack

of Coronas. He went out to the parking lot, locked the van and stood at the bus stop drinking his brews where he could have a good view of the intersection. While he acted like he was waiting on a bus, a balding, older-looking white man pulled up in a white Corvette. He motioned for Johnny to come to the window, and Johnny did, thinking that the man might need directions.

"Hey, man," the white dude began. "I got a drug test for my job tomorrow and I'm dirty. I'll pay you seventy-five dollars to piss in this cup."

"Naw, I'm cool," Johnny said.

The man pulled into the store's parking lot and asked a woman coming out. She went to the rear of the parking lot, on the other side of the van with the cup. Keeping a close eye on the van, Johnny could see the woman's silhouette through one of the tinted side windows as she raised her dress and whipped-out before filling the cup.

Oh, hell naw! He quickly turned his head and got back to his brew. A few minutes later, he saw the white man driving out of the parking lot, turning his cup up as he emptied the contents into his mouth.

What the fuck? I woulda beat his ass! he thought as he started toward the van. He walked past the fag who pissed in the cup. It was Marlon.

Kicking off his heels and holding down his wig, Marlon broke through the alley, pulling up his dress so his legs could stretch as he sprinted. Johnny threw a beer bottle at his head, but missed. Johnny then hopped into the van. As soon as he got to the alley, he saw Marlon hopping into a car with a trick, but there was no catching him since the traffic from a green light kept Johnny from pulling out of the alley.

Not only did Marlon escape, but now Johnny's cover was blown.

* * *

Mona rode with her friend, Goldie, to see a house that

Goldie was thinking about buying when Mona's phone rang.

"Who is that, girl" asked Goldie.

"Just some nigga I met at the bar," she lied, knowing it was Roy Jr. trying to get next to her. She had been dodging him every since she met him, but would give him small talk over the phone. He wanted to see her again and she knew it, but didn't want to risk being seen with the grimy individual. She'd told him her name was Kim to keep him that much easier to dispose of.

"See, girl, that's why I never fuck with niggas from the bar. It's always confusion."

"Yeah, you right. I might go out with him, though. See how much he's willin' to spend on me."

"I know that's right."

"Hello," Mona answered.

"Yo', this Roy. What's good with you?"

"Just chillin' with my girl."

"How long you gon' be doin' that? 'Cause me and my dogs 'bout to go bowlin' and I was tryin' to see if you wanted to roll with me for good luck."

"You can pick me up after I get done with my girl."

"Bet!"

Mona had Roy Jr. meet her at a store near Goldie's house. He pulled up bumpin' Cash Money.

"Hey," Mona said as she hopped into the Caprice.

"What's good with you? What happened to your girl? I had a few homies that wanted to meet her."

"They ain't never even seen her."

"I know, but they saw you, and think everybody you hang with is fine like you."

"I guess that's a compliment."

At the bowling alley, Mona sat back in the booth, watching as Roy and his homies bowled. Even though they were in Livonia where she knew she wouldn't know anyone, she still couldn't bring herself to mingle with Roy and his crew. Lubed from about four whiskey sours, Mona began to notice Roy's athletic build. She knew he was ugly as hell, but wondered how his body worked with the lights off. She knew he would really be on her if she allowed him a taste of the goods, but she was starting to tingle and wouldn't mind holding something thicker than Derek's frail frame, and didn't feel much like being smothered by Stone. It was time to open Roy's nose anyway.

Mona watched Roy as he repeatedly looked over at her to see if she was watching him, so she decided to blow his head up. She blew him a kiss when he looked again. It shocked him so much that he had to do a double-take. Inside she laughed but maintained a seductive look as Roy showed teeth. She mouthed, “Come here” and Roy dropped the bowling ball and came.

“How long y'all gon' be playin'?” she asked.

“Not too much longer. What's up?”

“I ain't tryin' to be with all yo' boys. I can't hang all night and wanted to chill with just you. But I understand if this y'all thang. I ain't tryin' to interfere with that.”

“Oh, don't even worry about it. If you ready, we can bounce. I'll see them niggas later!”

Smiling as if he'd just made her day, she asked, “Where you gon' take me when we leave here?”

Looking baffled, Roy said, “Shit, I don't really know. I ain't got too much loot left.” He looked down like he dropped his dignity.

“At least you keep it real. I like that.”

“That's 'cause I'm a real nigga,” he said while sticking his chest out.

“That's good 'cause I'm real, too. So, what you gonna do wit' a real chick like me?”

“Oh, I got you!”

“I hope so. Come here,” she said, digging into her small handbag. She pinched a hundred dollars off a small bankroll. She pressed it into his hands so that his boys could see, knowing they would work in her favor since they saw how down for him she was. Now she really had him glowing. “Here, boo. I got you, too,” she said, devilishly pouring the game on him thick, knowing that he would scale the Sphinx to rebuild the nose for her before being cut-off, having to suffer painful withdrawals on top of being called a damned fool by his boys for allowing her to slip away.

“What's this?” he asked with a goofy smile.

“Don't matter, you took it so you belong to me,” she said as she stepped to him, went in his pocket and pulled out his car keys. She finally got a chance to use her runway strut that she had practiced so many times growing up when she one day wanted to become a model. She glanced over her shoulder and saw him trailing behind like a puppy, like he was supposed to. She then put a little more umph into her stride, making her butt-cheeks rise and fall with rhythmic snap as she impregnated Roy's mind with thoughts of fornication.

She whipped up at a motel in Southfield and told Roy to pay for a short stay as she tossed him a fifty.

Inside the humble room, she saw that he was ready by the bulge in his pants, so she stripped right in the middle of the floor. “You gon' make me get under these covers by myself?” she asked as she crawled across the bed like a panther stalking its prey. Before she could get under the cover, he was undressed and on his way to the bed.

Roy laid pipe like a champ, but after a few minutes of sex, she couldn't stand to look into his face any longer so she told him, “Oooohh, you feel sooo good, daddy. I want to give it all to you. Let me turn over so you can handle yo' biz!”

“Damn!” he said, obviously bewitched by her form in the doggy-style position. After a few more thrusts, it was over.

Chapter 11

Johnny reclined in the back seat of Andre's Impala watching Marlon's apartment for activity. Dre was a younger thug from Johnny's hood who always tried to be down with Johnny. Johnny watched Dre as he grew up, but never thought he was worthy enough to put in work. Even when Dre tried to hang out and drink with Johnny and Ross, he was spun off.

Dre was a football player back in high school and still had a husky build. He was short and bald with a nutmeg complexion. He was known to put in work around the way, but to someone who had stripes like Johnny, Dre was still a novice.

With Johnny's cover blown, he let Dre roll to stay incognito in Dre's car.

After two hours with no sign of Marlon, Johnny's phone rang. "Yo," he said into the phone.

"What's up, baby?"

"Who dis?" he asked, thinking it was Ross's voice, but knew

Ross wouldn't be calling his new cell number with the heat on like it was.

"This Ross, playa!"

"What?"

"Be cool, nigga. I had Sonya three-way you. We straight."

"What you mean?"

"I mean I need a ride. Come get me, they dropped the charges."

"Straight up?"

"Yeah. Dig this: that young nigga, Ramone, killed his baby and his chick hisself. They say he took out a million-dollar life insurance policy on 'em. You know the insurance company wasn't tryin' to pay that shit so they had all kinds of hound-dog investigators on the case. I mean people was comin' up here askin' me shit every other day about what went down. Once they built a strong enough case, they took their shit to the prosecutor who put out a warrant for Ramone. They didn't drop the charges against us until that fool cracked under the interrogations."

"Damn, that's deep!" Johnny said as he smiled with relief. "So you ready, huh?"

"Man, quit playin' and get down here!"

"Take me to the van, playa!" Johnny told Dre.

"What's goin' on? You don't want to wait for ol' boy no more?"

"Not right now. I gotta swoop up Ross."

"They lettin' him out?"

"Yup."

On the way to Ross's van, Johnny purposely took the long route in order to ride past Benny's house. "That's where that rat-ass nigga live at that told on us." Johnny said as he pointed out Benny's crib to Dre.

"Straight up? I know y'all gon' handle that fool."

Johnny kept silent.

"Man, let me roll. I'll do that nigga. Y'all can just sit in the car."

"I ain't goin' near that nigga 'cause the po-po's will think it was Ross since he just got out. Ya feel me?"

Dre nodded and nothing else was said about Benny. "What you about to do?" Johnny asked as he hopped out of Dre's car. He hoped Dre would try to earn some stripes while he and Ross were still at the County.

"Probly just go and chill with my girl."

"That's good. I'll holla later." Johnny could see that Dre was in a hurry to get to something and hoped it would be Benny.

It took seven hours for Ross to finally come out with all the paperwork and processing at the County. On the way to Sonya's, Johnny filled Ross in on the incident with Marlon.

"What? You mean Toya gave you a shot of ass in my van to burn that nigga?"

"Yup! And you know Herb said he still got the spots for us at the plant if we ever beat the case."

"Well, we beat 'em, and I want to get in there pronto!"

"After bein' on the run, I'm 'bout ready to do that shit myself."

* * *

"How you gon' get mad at me?" Mona asked Stone the day after chillin' with Roy.

"'Cause you coulda called me back at least once." Stone wasn't as easy to manipulate as Derek and was beginning to want more and more of Mona's time and sex. He felt like even though she had a man, she should make more time for him since he was being so generous to her.

Mona had been dodging him every since he walked into the bar that day. That made Stone feel like she was trying to hide something, like she didn't want to face him. To kill her excuses, Stone told her to sit in the booth with him and gave her a hundred dollars for her time. He wanted to get to the bottom of things and she knew it.

"I told you this wasn't gonna work," she said to Stone. "I

don't even need to be doin' this. It's too much stress."

"So what you sayin'?" Stone asked.

"I'm sayin' we need to chill. I ain't 'bout to dump my man for you. You cool, but you're the type that think you can buy everybody, and soon as I leave my man for you, you'll be tryin' to keep me quiet with money while you fuckin' 'round with all kinds of ho's."

"You crazy. I was just tryin' to be with you, but if you wanna go, gone!"

"That's what I'm doin'," she said as she climbed out the booth she and Stone were in.

"And don't think I'm gon' hook up with you like I was doin' before either."

Mona put her hand on her hip. "I don't need your little plug. You know how many niggas be askin' me to move that shit for them?" Mona rolled her eyes and walked off. She knew Stone was too proud to allow her to just dump him like that. He was the type who wanted to do the dumping. Well aware of how Stone loved her sex, Mona knew he wouldn't sleep if she was getting dope from another nigga. He would automatically think the other guy was getting the sex he loved so much. So, for the rest of the night Mona ignored Stone, flirting and dancing extra freaky while he watched from across the room. She knew she couldn't get the price or quality of dope anywhere else, and hoped Stone would soon change his mind.

If he gave in and apologized, she would still be in charge of things and could continue to do as she pleased. But if she had to give in and come crawling back to him, he would demand more and more of her until he completely controlled the situation, and she wasn't trying to go out like that.

* * *

Sonya lay naked in bed with Johnny after their bedroom celebration for his name being cleared. Curled up in his arms, she talked on the phone to Gwen.

"I know you was happy to see Ross come home, too. Wait a

minute, girl. Turn to channel two! Ain't that the nigga that told on Ross and Johnny?"

"...Police detectives investigating a murder scene heard what sounded like a door being kicked in followed by gunshots from this house across the alley from the murder scene. After surrounding the house, they say an unidentified man came out shooting, so they returned fire, killing him instantly. Another man, identified as Benjamin Goode, was found dead inside from four gunshot wounds. Stay tuned to Channel Two news at ten for updates to this story..."

"See, girl. I'm so glad they ain't come in here shootin'. Damn, now I hate that we jumped that guy that day. Call auntie on the three-way so we can see if Herb still got them jobs for Ross and Johnny. I need to keep my boo out of trouble." She looked Johnny in the face, waiting for feedback.

Chapter 12

"Damn, playa. I can't believe Dre went out like that. I ain't think he had it in him," Johnny said to Ross as they creeped in the Impala looking for Marlon.

"Well, all he got in him now is slugs, 'cause they tightened his young ass up! I still can't wait to see this lame, Marlon dressin' up like a broad," Ross said as he sucked on the blunt.

"It's some crazy shit. I had been seein' him for a few days and didn't even know it was him."

"It must've really fucked his head up when you stole his girl."

"Naw. That wouldn't do that to him. He had to have that gay shit in him all the time. That fool think he's a broad for real."

"Is that him?" Ross asked as they crossed Woodward.

"Nope. That one is too short. He's damn near six-four in

heels."

Johnny navigated as Ross slowly whipped the small car around the Woodward and Six mile area. Johnny wanted to kill Marlon himself, but knew it might be better to let Ross handle it with his silenced nine-millimeter. They parked in the parking lot where Johnny saw Marlon before. Ross hopped out and hot wired an '84 Buick LeSabre. They left the bucket in the store parking lot and dipped through the alley to continue their hunt.

"Ride by Palmer Park. He probly on that stroll over there," Johnny told Ross.

At Palmer Park by the tennis courts, Johnny spotted Marlon hopping into the car of a young-looking white guy. "Look! There he go!"

After Ross finished holding his gut in a fit of laughter, he told Johnny, "When I get out, grab the wheel."

Once Ross grabbed the door handle to exit the vehicle, three unmarked police cars screeched to a halt behind the car Marlon was in. The officers jumped out and ran over and dragged Marlon out of the car. He kicked and screamed "Police brutality!" but they read him his rights and cuffed him. As they tried to walk him over to the squad car, Ross tried to ease the Buick past the arrest. Marlon made eye contact with Johnny.

"They tryin' to kill me!" Marlon shouted, nodding his head toward Johnny and Ross. "They got guns and stuff! Don't let 'em get away!"

Ross stomped the gas pedal when they saw one of the officers raise his walkie-talkie to his mouth. Before they knew it, they were in a high-speed chase.

Ross darted out into the Woodward traffic, pushing the LeSabre to its limit. After seeing the squad car gaining, he spun the wheel all the way left, hurdling over the island in the middle of Woodward. One squad car followed over the island while the other kept going to the turn-around.

"Shit!" Ross said as he turned the wrong way down a one-way street. They put some distance between the officers and themselves when they cut across another island.

"Blow through that alley!" Johnny told him.

As they rolled through the alley, they could hear the sirens getting closer. They stopped behind the store where they started, hopped into the bucket leaving the LeSabre's doors wide open. As they drove away doing the speed limit, they could see the officers hop out of their squad cars with guns drawn, approaching the abandoned stoley.

"Damn that was close," Ross said.

"Yeah, but you know that nigga gon' give up our names."

They looked at one another. Ross held the blunt while Johnny lit it.

* * *

Hey, boo. This Kim," Mona said to Roy a few days after hanging out with him.

She had played extra mad and extra hard to get when Stone approached her the night before to apologize, hoping he might reach into his pocket since he wanted her bad enough to give in.

"I really like you, Stone, but you're way too possessive. I can't deal with that right now."

"Just work with me; I can only try to do better," he told her.

"You sayin' that now 'cause you want some pussy. Next week it'll be back to the same thing." She turned to him and made eye contact. "Plus your temper is too bad. You act like you be wantin' to hit a bitch or somethin'. But if you ever put yo' hands on me, I'll have some niggas fuck you up!" She paused and waited for Stone's heated response.

"I ain't worried 'bout no punk-ass niggas!"

"See, that's what I'm talkin' 'bout! That's why I don't ever put my mouth on you!" She rolled her eyes as she turned, stomping away. She knew the thought of getting head would spark Stone's interest immediately.

"Man, wait up," he said while reaching for her arm.

"Let's talk about it, okay?"

"Stone, I gotta get home to my man."

The next morning, Mona went to Stone's for breakfast after telling Derek she was going to her mother's.

"You know I love you," Stone told Mona.

"If you loved me, I wouldn't have to catch a cab to get over here."

"You got a man. Tell him to buy you a car."

"Okay, I will. But don't think you gettin' none of his pussy when he do!"

"Oh, now it's all his pussy, huh?"

"Hell yeah! 'Specially if he gon' be gettin' me everything I need."

After a moment of thought, Stone said, "What if I let you grip the Infiniti?"

"That sound good," she said with a blush.

"See, that's what I'm talkin' 'bout; show that pretty smile. I'll drive the Benz and you keep the QX56 all day. Cool?"

"Yeah," she said with contentment in her voice.

"Now let's talk about that thang you brought up last night."

"What thang?" she said with a teasing blush.

"The head!"

"Oh, we gotta work on that like we gotta work on your temper and possessiveness, but when we get all that other stuff together, you can have it all your way." She quickly stripped and turned around. "You better catch me before I fall over," she said with her legs straight, reaching for her ankles before he had a chance to revoke her Infiniti priveledges.

Now after sexing Stone to sleep and spending the entire afternoon shopping and cruising around while doing her Kegels, Mona wanted to spend a little time with her stunt-dick. To Swoop him in the Infiniti, knowing it would only take him up higher, making him feel like he had some sort of link to the big time. He was ugly as sin, but gave her the best sex she'd had in a while.

"So, what you doin', baby?" she drawled.

"Just chillin' and thinkin' 'bout you," Roy said. "Where you at? It sound like you in a car."

"I'm on my way to get you. Give me your address."

Seeing a crowd of guys in front of Roy's house, Mona stabbed the Infiniti toward them before coming to a screeching halt. She laughed as they scattered.

"I was just playin', y'all" she said as she got out. "Hey, boo." She walked over and planted a kiss on Roy's cheek in front of his boys.

"Damn, nigga! Got it goin' on," the crowd said as they went wild.

"Who shit is this?" Roy asked.

"Why, you think I stole it?" Mona asked as she opened the door. "You ain't goin'?"

As Roy stood looking baffled, a little nappy-head hoodlum stuck his head out of the crowd. "I'll go!"

While snowflakes drifted from the Heavens, Mona drove by one of the clubs in Greektown. She parked and they watched people leaving the after work affair at the club.

"Damn, look at that mink ol' girl got on," Mona said.

"Oh, that's what you like, baby?"

"Cut it out! You ain't ready to get me nothin' like that," she said, running mind games like she didn't give a damn.

"Man, hold on! I'm Roy Jr., baby! Pull off." They drove in the opposite direction as the woman.

"What's up?"

"Let me out," he said as they approached the corner.

Once he hopped out, Mona bent the corner and came back around to see Roy with a gun to the mink-wearing woman's head, mustering his harshest bitch-I'll-kill-you face. After he yanked off her coat and jewels, he darted past Mona and around the corner. Mona went around the block again and picked him up in the alley.

* * *

The Sunday afternoon following the clearing of Ross and

Johnny's names, a celebration dinner was held at Sonya's. Johnny started drinking early, knowing that irritating Herb would be there. Johnny knew he had to put up with it if he wanted to get a spot at the plant.

As the family gathered at the table for a game of Spades, the doorbell rang. It was Mona and Derek.

"Hey, y'all," Mona said as she switched in her tight-fitting mini-skirt. She looked like a bootlegger's wife with her mink and sparkling jewels. Derek was even shining, flexing a white-gold pinky ring chocked full of glistening princess-cut diamonds.

"Damn, y'all blingin' today ain't y'all," Elisa joked. "You must be treatin' my baby good, Derek. She struttin' 'round in minks and what not."

"Well, I try," Derek said while hanging his hooded, three-quarter Pelle'-Pelle' in the front closet.

Johnny immediately got up and walked toward his bedroom. "Derek, let me holla at you for a second."

After closing the door, Johnny sat, still sipping on his drink. "Derek, what y'all been doin'?"

"What you mean, man?"

"I mean all that shit y'all got on make it look like you don't even owe Smurf no more. You take care of that yet?"

"Naw. I go holla at him in about two hours. He want to wait till it's about to get dark to hook-up. It's bad enough we be right in back of his record shop, so at least he try to keep anybody that happen to ride by from seein' what we doin'."

"Yeah, 'cause I know the people that live on the other side of that alley probly nosy as hell. I guess that make sense if he gon' do hot shit like that near his business in the first place."

"Yeah, he kind of smart 'cause everything is over in less than thirty minutes. I hate that wait, though. I'm glad I got some more cash comin' in."

"Oh, so you straight now?"

"Yeah. Got a new plug slangin' raw. My baby hooked me

up with some chick at the bar. That ho got the best dope any of my custos ever seen. And I got a few old-heads on my line that been 'ootin' heron since the early seventies."

"Twerkin' the dog food now, huh?"

"Hell yeah! It's startin' to flow, too."

"Just be careful. That's some serious shit. And the hook will be tryin' to bolt yo' ass up if you ever get knocked."

"I know. I just need to get my bread right now."

"It's all good. Let's get back out here with the family."

Johnny stopped drinking, knowing he and Ross had been waiting for the day when Smurf would re-up. He watched Ross happily playing cards. Ross was still getting his drink on, and would be ready to put in work whether he was lubed or not. He was always ready, so Johnny decided not to even tell him until it was time to move.

"So, Herb, you still got those jobs for us," Ross asked.

"Of course. I'm a man of my word. Y'all ready to go to work?"

"Yup! After sittin' in the County, wonderin' if I was ever gon' be free again, I'm definitely ready for that!"

"What y'all talkin' 'bout?" Mona asked.

"Oh, just some positions at the plant I promised these two," Herb answered.

"Why y'all ain't ask Derek? He need a job, too."

"I'm cool," Derek said.

"Well, right now I only have those two spots open," Herb said.

"Boy, you better get one of them good jobs while you can if you gonna be with my daughter," Elisa told Derek. "Baby, you think you can work something out for my son-in-law?" Elisa asked Herb with extreme tenderness.

"Aw, baby, you know as soon as something comes along, he'll be the first to get in. As a matter of fact, I'm sure one of you nice guys will be willing to let Derek go in your spot, wouldn't you?" Herb said to Johnny and Ross, no longer thinking about keeping his word, only thinking of pleasing Elisa.

"Naw, naw!" Elisa said. "Let them have the first spots. Keep your word. Something will come along for Derek. I just want you to remember him when it does."

"Damn, you was just gon' slice us out!" Johnny joked.

"Well it's nothing personal, young fella. But my baby does come first," Herb said as he turned love-sick eyes to Elisa.

Damn, she got that nigga sprung like a mu'fucka! Johnny thought.

After an hour and a half, Johnny raised from the card table. "Well, I think it's about that time, Ross."

Ross at first looked confused, but caught on after a few seconds. "Yeah, I ain't realize it was gettin' so late." He followed Johnny out to the van.

"Derek 'bout to hook up with Smurf. You got your burner with you?" Johnny asked.

"All the time," Ross said with enthusiasm.

Just as the horizon eclipsed the sun, Johnny and Ross arrived at the old cemetery on Lyndon and Meyers. Ross twisted the silencer off the nine so that the noise would civilize a crowd or anyone feeling heroic. Johnny had his trusty Mac-11 with the extended clip projecting from the pistol grip. He wasn't as good a shot as Ross, but knew that once he aimed and strangled the trigger, his Mac would hiccup pieces of hell.

They parked the van, snatched their ski masks from the glove compartment, then dashed through the maze of tombstones, through Butzel Field and the two blocks down Monte Vista until they neared Fenkell where Smurf's record shop sat.

"Let's dip through this backyard," Johnny said, pointing to the second house from the corner.

Once in the backyard, they could see nearly a dozen heads over the tall, wooden fence that separated the backyards from the alley behind the Fenkell storefronts.

"It look like it's 'bout twelve of 'em back there. They all gotta have at least twenty gees' apiece," Ross said as he gave Johnny some dap. "I'll come around from the front, and you trap 'em from behind." Ross sprinted back out onto Monte Vista.

Ducking down, Johnny went out to the alley that separated the backyard he'd been in from the yard the block over. Slipping on his ski mask, he took the alley two doors down to the point where it spilled into the alley behind the Fenkell storefronts where Smurf and his crew were gathered.

Johnny waited until he saw Ross in place before he stepped from the shadows. Ross didn't say a word, he just let his nine holla, dropping one of Smurf's boys. Everyone else reached for the stars as the two desperadoes closed in.

Just as Ross reached for Smurf, the back door to the shop swung open and a snail-faced goon jumped out with a pistol-gripped Mosberg. Johnny sent a stream of bullets his way. Snail-face went down. Then, *bucka, bucka, bucka* sounded from the roof.

Damn! Time to scatter, Johnny thought as he sprayed bullets toward the roof, scrambling back to the alley between the backyards.

As Johnny approached the van, the brake lights flashed as it jumped to life. Johnny hopped in the passenger seat and kicked back.

"Damn, that nigga had a mu'fucka on the roof!" Ross said as he stabbed the van onto Meyers.

"Yeah, I wasn't ready for that."

"I got one, though."

Johnny and Ross looked to one another and smiled.

Chapter 13

"Who did this to you, baby?" Mona asked Derek while at his bedside at Grace Hospital Monday morning.

"I was with Smurf. I think he set me up, tryin' to kill me for bein' so late with his money." Derek looked to Mona with an expression of overwhelming sadness. "I was tryin' to pay him, but he still tried to kill me!"

Until that moment Mona hadn't realized how attached she had become to Derek. He was her man. She cheated, but he was still her man. She knew right then just how much she really cared for him.

Some nights when she came in, it was obvious that he knew

she'd been out doing wrong, but he wouldn't say a thing, perhaps tired of the arguments and just wanted to make his thang work. Those were the nights he would just throw his arm around her and relax. Those were the moments that made Mona know that she had someone who really cared for her.

He wasn't her ideal dream-man, nothing like her deceased ex, and that was one of the reasons that in her mind Derek didn't meet her standards. She had been taking him for granted, and now while able to see to the bottom of her well, she didn't like the thought of having it go dry, thirsting for romance.

As Mona took an inventory of her love life, she mentally demoted Stone and Roy Jr. to the level of playthings that they actually were to her. Tears flooded her eyes as sorrow cascaded through her. She wanted her man well again so that she could enjoy with him all the things she had taken for granted before. She began to yearn for the loving feelings Derek gave her, for the stability he offered. As she looked to the shit-bag hitched to Derek's side, she could feel her eyes narrow to irrigating slits from the fury storming inside her.

She was a powerful woman, and Smurf had tried to pulverize her happy home, tried to disintegrate the wonderful, fairy tale dream that every girl has.

That wasn't cool.

* * *

Sonya eased her small Honda down McNichols on her way to pick up Gwen. They were going to meet Mona at the hospital while she sat with Derek.

Knowing how loose Mona was, Sonya thought that she might soon get tired of sitting there with him alone. So, she and Gwen decided to hang out at the hospital with Mona, to keep her up there with her man longer.

Sonya was happy that Mona and Derek hooked up, not just because she wanted Mona from under her roof, but because she felt like Derek might somehow be able to keep Mona out of trouble.

After scooping Gwen, the two stopped at a liquor store to grab some vodka. They filled their cups in the store parking lot, then got back on McNichols.

"Yeah, girl. She say somebody just came out the bushes tryin' to rob Derek and all his boys. I'm glad Johnny wasn't hangin' with him that night," Sonya said.

"I know that's right. Ross just got back home, too," Gwen said while giving Sonya some dap. As soon as their fists touched, they hit something.

"Aaaagh!" Sonya screamed as a woman flipped up onto the hood, hitting her head on the windshield.

"Go, go!" Gwen shouted.

"No! We gotta stop!"

"We can't wait for no white police to come and we been drinkin'!"

Knowing that Gwen was right, Sonya floored the small machine, sending the woman rolling off onto the pavement and into the path of oncoming traffic. After hitting a few corners, they took sidestreets all the way to the Southfield service drive, then creeped to Eight mile and took that to Sonya's apartment complex.

They stashed the car under the parking shelter and ran into the apartment.

Sonya's hands shook as she spun the cap off the vodka bottle. "Damn, I can't believe she ran out into traffic like that! What was she thinking about?"

"I don't know, girl. My heart is poundin'. Pour me another shot, too."

"We need to call Johnny and Ross. They'll know what to do. That was a big bitch!"

"Yeah, you ain't lyin'."

Sonya's heart still pumped nitro as she grabbed the phone to call a cab. "Let's just get up there to chill with Mona, then we can tell Johnny and Ross later. And we leavin' that car here!"

"I know that's right! I kinda wonder who she was."

Sonya drained her cup. “I do, too, but not enough to go back!”

* * *

“Hello,” Johnny said into his cellphone. He and Ross were on their way to see Derek at the hospital. Knowing that their positions were secure at the auto plant, they went a day after Sonya and Gwen, thinking that Elisa would have been with them with Herb in tow. And the thought of being cooped up in a small room with Herb's flapping gums irritated Johnny to the core. Plus, after finding out about Derek, they were certain that Ross's bullet hit Derek. And they knew they would be eaten alive by guilt, and didn't want the ladies to see it on their faces.

“Yeah, this Toya.”

“Oh, what's up with you?”

“I thought you was gon' put ol' boy at the top of your priority list?”

“I did, but I been goin' through some shit tryin' to handle that. I ain't even seen him in the last few days.”

“That's 'cause he at the hospital, in a coma.”

“Straight up?”

“Yup! Some bitch hit him with her car and kept goin'.”

“You lyin'!” Johnny said thinking of Sonya and Gwen.

“Nope. Happened yesterday on Six mile. He was in drag and everything. Now he's in room five-eleven. So, can you do it or not?”

“Fo' sho'! It's done,” he said as he shut off his phone. “Ross, I think that was Marlon Sonya and Gwen hit yesterday.”

“Why you say that?”

“'Cause Toya just told me that he's in a coma 'cause some chick hit him with her car.”

“Oh, so he just layin' there helpless?” Ross asked, obviously more concerned with doin' Marlon than assumptions about the ladies' events behind the wheel. “We can get his ass while he sleep!”

They u-turned and stopped at a resale shop where Johnny

purchased a stethoscope along with cook's smock. He slipped his sweatshirt off, then put on the smock. He pulled his shirt over the smock.

Since Derek was in the same hospital as Marlon, they got back on course to Grace hospital.

After getting two visitor passes, they went up to spend time with Derek.

Thirty minutes into the visit, with the stethoscope up his sleeve, Johnny got up to go to the van. He hopped on the elevator, trying to remember Marlon's room number. *Damn, I think it was five-something.*

The elevator door opened on the fifth floor, and Johnny peeked his head out, looking both ways to make sure the coast was clear. He slipped into an open supply closet. Inside, he took off his shirt and stashed it behind some cleaning supplies, then placed the stethoscope around his neck. A clipboard fell to the floor as he backed into a small cart. He grabbed the clipboard, thinking it would enhance his costume. Knowing he looked ridiculous in a too-small cook's smock with Nikes and French braids, he started out to find his victim.

He could hear female voices, possibly nurses, coming from around the corner. He peeked into the first room he came to. An old fat woman sat with her graying spouse, and in the other bed was a dude missing an arm. The next room was occupied by a skeletal white man, probing his nostril with a forefinger.

Johny could hear wheels squealing over a group of voices. He ducked into the skeleton's bathroom as the nurses wheeled their patient by. As he came out, the skeleton spoke.

"Doctor, are you here to change my catheter?"

"Uh, no. A nurse will be by shortly to do that," Johnny said as he glanced at the clipboard at the foot of the skeleton's bed.

He peeked out of the room, then continued on his mission. The corner where the voices once were was now quiet, so he went around it, checking each room along that hallway. Finally, he came to a wing where everyone seemed to be in critical condition, hooked up to life support with breathing machines and all sorts of tubes and IV's jabbed into their bodies. He got to the third room, and noticed that a woman was on her way to the restroom. He turned and looked to his clipboard until he heard the restroom door close behind her. Then, he tiptoed into the room.

The name on the clipboard at the foot of the bed was Hill. *Hell yeah! Finally!* The man in the corner bed seemed to be a vegetable or at least in a coma also, so Johnny crept to Marlon's bedside. He kicked the plugs to the machines surrounding Marlon's bed from their socket's, politely lifted Marlon's chin, and focused his strength into a Karate chop that left no trace of Marlon's Adam's apple.

Johnny heard the toilet flush, and sprinted out the door, down the hall, around the corner, past the group of nurses wheeling a patient on a bed, and into the supply closet.

He quickly changed, then went back to Derek's room. Derek had fallen asleep.

"Psst, Ross," Johnny whispered. "Let's dip."

Chapter 14

Elisa stood in the kitchen dicing green peppers and onions for Herb's steak, listening to the rundown of Ross and Johnny's first day on the job.

"I think they'll do well. They seemed to know a lot of people already," Herb told her.

"I still wonder what those boys where doing before this. They seemed to have enough money for whatever they needed. Did they ever tell you anything about any other jobs?"

"No. Not that I can remember," he answered while rubbing his chin.

"It's kind of funny the way Sonya dodged the question anytime I asked her about how they made their livings. I'll bet it was something illegal."

"Well, baby, they have good jobs now."

"Still no word on a job for Derek? You know he only has a few more weeks before the doctor says he'll be well again."

"No, not yet. But I'll definitely let you know first," Herb said as he moved to hug Elisa from behind.

"Yeah, because he is with my daughter, and I don't like the

thought of that nice boy messing around in them streets, turning out like Mona's last boyfriend."

"I don't think you'll have to worry. Johnny asked the foreman about it already."

"What does that mean? He just started today. He don't have the kind of pull to get Derek a job." Elisa still worked on Herb's meal while in his embrace.

"I wouldn't say that. The foreman who was giving them their tour of the plant seemed to be scared of him for some reason, like maybe he knew them, too."

Elisa dropped the knife and turned her head to meet Herb's eyes. "Scared of him? What would a grown man be doing scared of him?"

"I-I don't know," Herb stammered, now acting as if he said something wrong. "The guy just treated them with a lot of respect like they were mob bosses or something."

"Well, how does he normally act? How does he treat everybody else?"

"That's the thing, the guy's usually an asshole. Everybody in the plant hates him. He was smiling and what not around those two like they were the ones who signed his checks or something."

"Oh, is that right?" Elisa shook her head, then went back to fixing Herb's meal. "It's definitely something there that I don't like."

"I don't think that's really a problem. It's probably just because it was their first day on the job."

"Well, keep me posted."

"You know I will, baby," Herb said like a well-mannered child.

"You said the other employees acted like they knew them. Were they treating Johnny and Ross with the same respect as that foreman?"

"Yeah, come to think of it, they were. And those women were...man!"

Elisa pushed Herb back off her. "Were what, Herbie?!"

"Oh, I mean they were all on those guys like groupies on rappers."

"What?" Elisa dropped everything in her hands again and placed her hand on her hip.

"I said they acted like they already knew them."

"You didn't say they had women all over them and everything!"

"Well--"

Elisa picked up the knife and pointed it at Herb. "You better keep me posted on everything that goes down in that place! You understand me?"

"Yeah, baby. I told you I would."

"Those boys better not be down there fooling around on my babies!"

"Think we can fool around a little?" Herb asked as Elisa placed the steak into the oven.

She pushed past him. "Move outta my way!"

* * *

The second day on the job, Johnny ducked in and out of cars flowing down the assembly line, checking to make sure all the lights were working. He knew he had a job that most of the employees in the plant wanted because it didn't involve back-breaking work. He got that hook-up due to Sonny being the plant manager.

Sonny was an African-American who was raised in a home with both parents. Sonny and Johnny both attended Cooley High school where Sonny maintained good grades. Growing up, he had the Polo shirts and Guess jeans, always had something to spend which he received from his parents.

Johnny had to hustle and steal for his. Sonny was on the scene many a time when Johnny knocked brothers out for their 951 Gazelles, so Sonny knew just how ruthless Johnny could be. Back then, to avoid being checked in, Sonny would make sure Johnny had the answers to the critical tests to pass his courses. As a result, Sonny always got a pass.

Now, after fifteen years, a few college degrees and experience in the cruel world, Sonny maintained his same attitude, making sure Johnny was content in his surroundings.

That first day, while Johnny was being escorted to his work assignment, he was taken to the assembly line where the new employees usually started. Sonny saw the way Johnny cringed at the power tools and hard labor that were prevalent there and took him to an area where he would be an inspector instead.

Sonny was well aware of the fact that when he got off work, the parking garage where his car was stored would be full of gloom and shadowy spots. With an unhappy Johnny on the premises, the walk past those murky corners would create fear and stress that would ultimately devour Sonny's peace of mind and sense of security. No one wanted to live like that. So, once again Sonny made sure Johnny was in a peaceful state of mind, happily jumping in and out of cars on the slow moving line.

The baddest bitches in the plant choked the small section. Most of them payed the admission to the area with their pussies.

Johnny loved his position since the work was easy and the women treated him like a kingpin, even the ones that didn't know him. And they probably thought he was a big-time drug dealer since he scored such a coveted spot on his first day. All day long the females jumped at the chance to help him in any way and just pamper him with flirty gestures. Johnny wanted to splash on cologne while dressing for work that morning, but knew he would have to cuss Sonya out for talking shit about other chicks.

One of the women he worked with was twenty-four, and used to pass him while he and his boys hustled on her block early mornings as she went to school. Her name was Nikki, and she was a hammer. Her body was pear-shaped with a small waist and exploding hips and ass. Her hair was cut low and her eyes were beautiful pools of peace, round with pretty black pupils.

Back in the day, she and her friends called Johnny, Mr. Clean for the fresh gear he wore while on the grind. Back then she was too young for Johnny, but now she was full grown, wonderfully developed with wicked lips that looked like they could suck him into next month.

"Hey, Mr. Clean," Nikki flirted with a smashing smile.

"What's up, girl. I see you all grown up now."

"Yeah, it happens. So, how you like your new job?"

"It's cool. Not too hard."

"Bet you ain't never work before a day in yo' life. I remember y'all out on the corner back in the day when me and my girls was goin' to school. Up early gettin' money."

"Yeah, them was the good old days."

"I bet they was. Back when you wouldn't give a sista a chance."

"A chance for what?" he said with a blush.

"Cut it out, man! You know I always had a crush on you."

"How was I supposed to know that?"

"Okay, smarty pants. Play them games. You just got here and I bet you already got half the women in the plant chasin' you."

"Naw, I ain't nowhere."

"You ain't nowhere?"

"Nope." Johnny took a deep gaze into her eyes and reaped do-it-to-me vibes that made his dickhead sore from bulldozing the inner wall of his jeans.

"I'm twenty-one today, and I had the day off, but came in 'cause I saw you yesterday."

"You should let me take you to lunch."

"You gon' buy me a drink after you feed me?"

"Yeah, I got you."

"Good, 'cause it's my birthday, and I wanna get fucked..."

"I got you!"

"...Up!"

* * *

Ross stood on a platform jabbing buttons on a control panel in the paint shop. He "somehow" lucked up and landed a gravy position that kept him from ever breaking a sweat.

To him, the plant was a small state with each work area being a separate city. His was the ghetto, plagued by drug dealers and number runners. He felt at ease after scanning the area for enemies he might've had beef with in the past. He'd noticed yesterday, during his lunch break, a red Monte Carlo in the parking lot with a line of people hopping in and out. Most of the people in line were young, his age or younger. Ross knew that it had to be the weedman.

He knew the street numbers were generating just as much cash as the dope after witnessing an old-head stopping at every work station and assembly line, jotting things down on a small pad before collecting cash, then moving on to the next person or work area.

Ross wondered what department the numbers guy was assigned to, and how he could just roam around like he was doing without a foreman jumping down his throat.

Ross tried not to get distracted by the fine women who had asses bulging even through cover-alls. He knew a few from around the way, but felt like he should concentrate more on the ones that might be from the east side or somewhere to keep word of his cheating from reaching Gwen. 'Cause he could already see cheating in his very near future.

He had his eye on a full-figured girl with chinky eyes. Her name was Felicia, and Ross knew she sold heroin because every one of the people who ventured to her from surrounding areas for slick money exchanges would go to a secluded spot to nod off soon after.

Felicia had hair like an Indian and couldn't seem to keep her eyes off Ross. Knowing she was on him, he tried to ignore her, seeing just how far she would go.

Once lunchtime finally rolled around, Ross felt something brush against his behind. He quickly turned to face Felicia's cheeky smile.

"Sorry 'bout that," she said.

"You know that's sexual harassment?" Ross joked.

"You gon' press charges?"

"I ain't say that. I just asked if you knew."

"Hold on a minute," she said as she turned and made a few quick money exchanges.

Ross saw their boss charging over toward them and tried to get her attention. "Felicia!"

She looked up and paid the boss no mind.

"Felicia," the boss began. "I was tryin' to catch you before you went on break."

Ross watched in amazement as she served their boss a blow. She whispered something in his ear before he hurried off.

"So what you doin' for lunch?" Felicia asked Ross.

"I ain't got no plans. What about you?"

"Whatever you wanna do. We got a extra hour."

"We do?"

"You with me, ain't you?"

"Oh, you got it like that?"

She stepped close to Ross. "I feel like I do 'cause I'm with you. You thc hot boy."

"You don't know nothin' 'bout Ross-dog."

"I heard 'bout when you robbed Black."

"How you hear 'bout that?" Ross asked, thinking he was on top of his game when he made Black disappear some years earlier.

"I used to kick it with the nigga that was workin' the spot when you ran up in it."

"Is that right? What else do you know?"

"I know you be out there gettin' all the money and all the pussy."

"Is that right?"

"Yup!"

"Well, you got some money?"

She seductively batted an eyelash. "Nope!"

Chapter 15

Herb sat in his Cadillac STS in the plant's parking structure sipping Brandy and listening to the old-school jams over the radio. He was trying to make up his mind as to whether or not he should do like Elisa said and keep her posted on Ross and Johnny's ways. He knew if they were getting their groove on, Elisa could never find out. They surely wouldn't tell if he didn't. He knew that a large number of married people at the plant have had some sort of an affair at one time or another, and Ross and Johnny wouldn't be any different, especially with the reaction they were getting from the women. And neither one was married anyway.

Herb thought about the impact his report could have on the men's homes. Their relationships would certainly be over. Especially with the long hours most of the men worked. Their wives would never trust them again as long as they worked there. He just didn't want that on his conscience, because even if the two were out of the family, Herb would still have to see them most days at work. And they would know how the info escaped the plant and made it to their women.

Herb looked up to see Johnny escorting the young chick from quality control to her car. She had an arm around his waist, but he had a hand full of her giggly ass, squeezing it like Herb wished he could. Johnny stopped at the door of her GMC Envoy, stuck his tongue in her mouth, then opened the door for her.

Herb was parked a few rows over, but had a clear enough view to tell that Johnny undid his pants before he crawled into that backseat after the young woman. Herb hit the Brandy, then cracked his window. For about ten minutes, he watched the truck rock rhythmically from side to side before the windows shaded white with fog. Her squeals echoing inside the structure made Herb so horny that he wanted to whip out and beat his dick. But, he knew if he got caught by anyone, the rep of being the plant perv would stick like duct tape.

Johnny didn't seem to give a damn who came along. He was in there gettin' buck wild, and seemed to be having so much fun doing it.

Herb's mind flashed back to the scene of Elisa with squinted eyes, pointing the butcher's knife at his chest. He had promised to tell her.

What if she somehow found out? He could wind up in just as much trouble as Johnny if Sonya found out, and Herb wasn't even gettin' buck wild. *Naw, naw, can't have that! I don't know what I'd do if my baby left me!*

Elisa was his friend, his adviser, his lover, his right hand, his financial planner and his soul mate.

Worse than being lonely would be loneliness after having had Elisa's love, and worse yet is loneliness while another received Elisa's love. Herb knew how cold-blooded her lovin' was to him and knew if another man ever got a hold of it, that man would never want to let it go.

Naw, naw, I can't have that!

* * *

With Derek getting better, Mona had been going back to work at the bar, but was growing tired of it. She had lost her zest for the brass poles and tricks. She felt a lot better when she was at home with Derek.

Now, she had to almost force herself to go to work. She had come to realize that stripping, selling her ass, working the night scene, wasn't the happening thing, just a bullshit gig like a drive-thru window with arctic winds gusting in, or a newspaper route in the dead of winter, pieces of her soul being traded for pennies.

That type of life wasn't one that could be worked until the age of retirement. Self-degradation at its worse.

She had only wanted to dance temporarily, a stepping stone until she could reach the next level. She knew now was the time to reach for the way out. But, before she left, she had loose ends to tie.

Mona had already informed Stone of Derek's injury, so he figured he could get that much more of her time while Derek was recovering, thinking Derek was still laid up in the hospital.

Roy Jr. knew Mona had a man, but didn't know who he was.

"Roy, I'm going to be riding with my boyfriend tonight," Mona whispered into her phone as she crouched in a bathroom stall at the bar. "I just want to do this thing so we can be together. You know how I feel about you. Okay, so be on the lookout for the Infiniti with me in the passenger seat. I came in early, so I'll be leaving at about eight. We'll be going to the address I told you about.

"We got to do this right, so you gotta be rough with me so he won't think nothin'. No, don't worry, he won't have anyone in the car with us. He don't trust none of his boys, 'specially 'round me. Okay, I love you, bye."

Mona went out onto the stage and danced until she stood on a blanket of green, then made rounds giving lap dances. At seven-thirty, Stone walked in. Thirty minutes after that, Smurf walked in.

Mona had been trying to spin Stone as much as possible without pissing him off, just enough to make him jealous. Smurf coming in was just the thing she needed. She wanted to get closer to him anyway.

"What's up, baby?" Mona asked Smurf as he drained a champagne bottle.

"Oh, it's you? Gimme a dance."

"What you mean, it's me? You know me?" she asked, hoping he hadn't somehow associated her with Derek.

"No, I don't know you, but I would like to. I just remember the last time I got a dance from you. I ain't seen you since."

"I been around."

"Not in here, 'cause I was lookin'."

"And what was you gon' do if you found me?" she asked while doing a handstand, spreading her legs so Smurf could see the greedy beast in the middle devouring her bikini string.

Smurf's lower jaw dropped in amazement. "Wha-what? Oh! Oh yeah! I was just gon' see if we could go someplace where we could maybe dance together instead of you doin' all the dancin'."

Mona got back on her feet in time to see Stone gazing with murderous eyes from across the room. Mona winked at him. She then got her money from Smurf and turned to walk away.

"Hold on!" Smurf said. "What you think about what I said?"

"Oh, the dance? I don't know, just give me your number so I can talk to you about it." She sat in the booth next to him to keep Stone from seeing her get the number. "I gotta get ready to go. My ride is here," she said as she rose to her feet and did her runway walk toward Stone, knowing Smurf was watching from the rear.

"What was all that?" Stone asked.

Mona knew he wasn't going to trip after the falling out they had before, so she played it off. “Just some new moves I been workin' on. What's up with you, baby?”

“Naw, don't try to change the subject! I wanna know why I ain't get to see them new moves.”

“You just did.”

“Oh, I don't get the new dance?”

“Boy, quit it! You know you 'bout to get all the new moves when we get to yo' house.”

* * *

“I'm so proud of my baby,” Sonya said to Gwen as they chilled at Sonya's. “He said he like his new job.”

“Yeah, that's what Ross said, too. He even said they got some overtime comin' up. I don't know what he was doin' before he started at the plant, but now I feel so much better with him workin' there.”

“I know what you mean, girl. Every minute while I was at work, I used to always think Johnny was with other women. He still could be in there, but I don't think he'll have the energy after doin' all the hard work they got for him up in there. And with me puttin' it on him, he won't be able to do nothin' but sleep when he not workin', and that's good, 'cause he'll stay out of trouble!”

“I know that's right! I was about to go crazy when Ross was locked up. I know Mona will be glad when Herb get Derek in there, too.”

“Girl, Mona ain't thinkin' 'bout Derek.”

“Huh?”

“That girl be at work doin' her thang. I know for a fact she got at least two niggas that be comin' through the bar.”

“You lyin'!”

“Nope! And she'll probably be worse if Derek was gone to work all day.”

“Well, maybe it would be good if she got a job in there, too. She slowed down with her last boyfriend. I don't think she ran around on him at all.”

“Well, she runnin' a marathon with Derek. One of the girls saw her drivin' some niggas car. She could do just as bad in the plant. Think about all the people in there at once. It's like a small little world in there.”

“I better not find out Ross in there fuckin' 'round. Girl, we'll be fightin'!”

“I know that's right!” Sonya's words began to sink into her own mind as she realized the vast possibilities for Johnny to get down while at work. “I'm just gon' have faith in my man on this one. Ain't no way I would be able to find out the truth if somethin' was goin' on in there anyway. It's better to not even think about it.”

“You the one that brought it up.”

“I was talkin' 'bout Mona. Not my boo. I was sayin' good thangs about him 'cause he doin' so good right now.”

“Yeah, I trust Ross, but I'll keep my ears open when I'm 'round auntie. 'Cause I know if it's there, she gon' get it outta Herb's ass!”

Chapter 16

“Wait a minute,” Johnny said to Nikki as they exited the parking garage.

”What's wrong?” Nikki asked.

“Ol' boy know my girl.” Johnny pointed to Herb who was walking back into the plant. “I don't want him to see me right now.”

“You mean, you don't want him to see you with me, right?”

“Something like that.”

“Keep it real, baby.”

“I always do. That's why I told you 'bout her before.”

“It's all good. Are you rough with her like you was with me? You got my shit sore as hell!”

“I bet it ain't too sore for yo' man to get it tonight,” Johnny said as they began walking toward the plant again.

“I told you, I don't have one of those. Why you worried anyway?”

“I ain't worried.”

“I guess not. You got yours,” Nikki said with a smile.

“I just wanted you to have a good time on your birthday.”

“Oh so I won't be able to see you no other time? Only if it's my birthday?”

“I ain't say that. You puttin' words in my mouth.”

“How is it gon' be then?”

"What you mean?"

"You know what I mean. How is it gon' be with us? Will I get to chill with you sometimes after work, or is this somethin' you just tryin' to do on your lunchbreaks?"

"We can chill; that sound good."

"Okay, don't have a sista lookin' fo' ya!"

Johnny thought for a minute as Nikki switched her way to the timeclock. He knew the verbal contract he'd just entered meant to her that she had dibs on him.

She was strapped-the-fuck-up, had a cute face, and the hit was superb, but he didn't know if he should already be restricting his opportunities to hit other women in the plant. His new job was a surplus of thick, bad bitches, and he had just given boasting rights to one he could've hit in the hood.

There were chicks he hadn't even seen yet, and would more than likely be seeing new ones for the next few months. The plant was just that huge. And he had only experienced his small portion of it. He knew he needed to do more exploring before making decisions like that.

The way Nikki caught him off guard with her questioning was slick as eel shit, but he knew that's how women were. *I bet it ain't even that ho's birthday!*

Back on the job, Johnny was constantly in the company of some woman. It became very clear to him that the other women must've seen him leaving with Nikki, and from the looks of things, none liked her. He had no feelings for Nikki, and if a rivalry was really going on, it could mean more pussy than he could handle.

* * *

Mona puffed a blunt with Stone on their way down Eight mile. They turned onto Greenfield and Mona began to wonder if she was making the right choice.

Stone was major and had killers on his payroll, and if he ever found out she'd double-crossed him, her blue-ribbon pussy wouldn't be enough to save her. The best part of it all was

Stone's distrust for his crew.

They turned down Vassar and her heartbeat increased. Even though she devised a plan she knew would work from experience, she was still scared as hell. She didn't know for sure what Roy would be driving, or if he would be alone or not. After not seeing any other cars on the sidestreet, she felt relieved thinking that maybe he'd chickened out.

They passed Prevost, then out of nowhere, a rear impact sucked her skull into the headrest. She quickly turned to see a van behind them with no lights on. *He made it!*

"What the fuck!" Stone shouted. "I'm 'bout to fuck somebody up!" He reached under his seat and whipped out a .45 automatic.

"Be careful," Mona shouted as Stone stormed out of the vehicle.

She turned to see Stone with his hands in the air. They got the drop on him.

Two masked bandits were approaching him fast. One had a shotgun, while the other had two pistols. Mona faked a scream, then cracked her window.

"Get yo' ass on the ground, nigga!" one of the masked men said. He produced a set of handcuffs and secured Stone's hands behind his back. He moved to Mona's door and snatched her out. After cuffing her hands, he tossed her back in her seat and got behind the wheel. The other masked man helped Stone off the ground and pushed him into the backseat. He squeezed in next to him. The Infiniti's tires squealed as they stabbed off.

"Man, what y'all want?" Stone asked.

"I wanna kill you if I don't get paid," said the driver.

"I got 'bout two gees' in my pocket; you can have it all," Stone bargained.

"Naw, playa. We want the real money and all the work."

"What y'all talkin' 'bout?" Stone asked.

"You'll see in one minute," the man next to Stone said. They whipped up into the driveway of Stone's safehouse and stabbed the car to the backyard which was surrounded by a tall wooden fence, then hopped out and closed the gate so no one on the street could see.

* * *

"So why you askin' me so many questions 'bout the rest of the plant," Felicia asked Ross while they sat in his van. They were on the long seat in back watching television. "Seem like you would be askin' me 'bout me." She looked at him as if she awaited a response.

"I'm just tryin' to find out how it is in there. You know I got the hook-up for you," Ross told her, not really having the hook-up, but knowing he could get it. He figured that since it was so much going on around there, he wanted in, and she was the perfect place to start.

"Do you?"

"All day long. What you gettin' when you get on?"

"Just a eight-ball. Sometimes a quarter-ounce, it depend on how good it is. Now, what kind of hook-up you got for me?"

Knowing he wasn't as experienced with heroin as with cocaine, he said, "Well see, that's small time. I thought maybe you was gettin' somethin' bigger."

"No, 'cause I only get down in the plant. So I only get what I need for in there."

"Well, I'll have to put somethin' together for you. I don't usually even go that low no more. I'm just gon' do this 'cause it's you, so don't go tellin' nobody 'bout yo' plug 'cause I ain't gon' work it for nobody else."

"You still ain't give me no numbers."

"I know. And I ain't right now. Let me know when you ready to get on again, then I'll take into consideration how nice you was to me."

"Oh, it's like that?"

"You ain't know? It's always like that. You bought me lunch today, and that was cool, but don't be tryin' to get evil on me later on 'cause I'll be watchin'."

"Listen to you! You the one with the woman!"

"And I ain't gon' leave her 'cause she rode with me while I was locked up. But that don't mean we can't be friends." Ross threw his arm around Felicia and slid closer. He paused to see her reaction, if she felt comfortable or not, but she leaned into him, so he slid his other hand over on her leg.

"Well, I'll need a quarter tomorrow for sure."

"Bet!"

"So, what was you locked up for?"

"Murder, but I beat the case." Remembering the sex with his ex who was just a little larger than Felicia made his dick hard as a tombstone.

"And how did I know that?"

"I don't know. How did you know?"

"That's the type of niggas I always fall for."

With his hand up her shirt stroking the ring of goosebumps around her nipple, he asked, "What kind of niggas is that?"

"Niggas that ain't shit!" Her eyes were now closed, seeming to Ross as an invitation to further his advances.

"Damn, I ain't know all that!"

"Oh, you knew, nigga, but it's cool. I just like thug-ass niggas."

Ross slid his hand from under her shirt.

She opened her eyes. "What's wrong?"

Ross stood with his head pressed against the van's ceiling.

"Oh, you mad 'cause I said you wasn't shit?"

He dropped his zipper. "I ain't mad. We still cool. I think you know I like you, but you gotta be nice to yo' new friend," he said as he whipped out stone love.

"And I guess I'm s'posed to suck it?"

"Man, come here." He grabbed her hand and pulled her out of her seat. She fell to her knees and gripped him like she couldn't wait to show what she could do with a dick.

She looked up into his eyes, then dropped her head. "Just like a nigga!"

Chapter 17

Johnny hopped into a car, switched on the lights, and before he could get out a chick hopped in on the passenger side.

"Hey," she said with a smile.

"What's goin' on?"

"I was only speaking. I know you just started and I wanted to make sure you felt welcome to our area."

"Oh, okay."

"My name is Marilyn, but you can call me Lynn." Lynn stood five-seven, was thick as peanut butter with a size twelve waist, had sandy skin and a small gap between her two fronts.

"I'm Johnny."

"So I heard."

"Gossip goin' 'round 'bout me already?"

"Nothin' bad. Just girl talk."

"Sound like some stuff I might wanna hear."

"Maybe I'll tell you 'bout it later." She hopped out and dashed back to her spot in the plant and got back to work.

Johnny looked over at Nikki who was shaking her head as if she were disgusted with him. By quitting time, he'd met four more females, all wanting to welcome him into the plant.

Once Johnny got to the time clock, Nikki was posted up waiting, trying to look occupied by playing with her cellphone.

"Waiting for me?" Johnny asked.

"Oh, naw. I was just tryin' to find a number in my phone."

"'Bout to get into somethin', huh?" he asked.

"I need to. It's my birthday, remember?"

"Oh yeah, that's right."

"See, you ain't nothin'. You forgot about me already."

"You know I ain't forgot that quick. I was just tryin' to see if you could take a joke."

"Oh really? So what you waitin' for?" she asked with her hand on her hip as if she thought it would be another female.

"My boy. I rode with him."

"Yeah, right. You 'bout to hook up with one of these ho's in here. I'll leave and get out yo' bizness." She turned to walk away with her face looking all tore up.

Johnny didn't give a damn. He watched her slowly walk away. He knew she expected him to stop her, to give some kind of explanation, but he didn't bulge, hoping that she could see a breach in their contract and expect nothing from him. He didn't really want to be on her bad side, but didn't want any obligations or commitments either.

As soon as Nikki vanished around the corner, Ross appeared, slow-stepping with a heavyset chick like they were in love. From the looks of it, Ross got a few points, too. Johnny never thought that maybe Ross would get as lucky as he. It wasn't the same kind of luck Johnny liked, but since Ross kind of liked big girls, he got down.

"What's up," Ross began. "This is my new friend, Felicia. She work over in my world."

"Damn, y'all got y'all own little world?" Johnny asked.

"How many of y'all started yesterday?" Felicia asked.

"Just us two," Johnny replied.

"That's good."

"Why you say that?" Ross asked.

"That'll make it easier to tell who the gossip will be about," Felicia said, her face beaming promise.

"What gossip?" Ross asked.

"Oh, they'll find somethin' 'round here, believe me!" Felicia replied.

Johnny walked behind Ross and Felicia after they punched out. Once they got outside, Johnny noticed Nikki, acting like she was consumed by conversation on her phone. By Johnny now being so far behind Ross and Felicia, he realized that to Nikki, it might appear that he was lying, like he was trying to shake her. *She ain't got no bizness stalkin' a nigga anyway!*

He faked like he didn't see her and kept walking. He could see Ross up ahead parting ways with Felicia as she went to her car. Then, he noticed Lynn talking with another female. Johnny tried to act like he didn't see her either, heading toward Ross who was waiting for him to catch up.

"What y'all 'bout to get into?" Lynn asked.

"The crib--" Johnny jumped as he felt a pinch on his ass.

"Alright now, Mr. Clean," Nikki said as she switched past.

"Damn, I better let you gone on," Lynn said.

As Johnny caught up with Ross, Ross asked, "What was all that?"

"Just some people in my world."

"Well, I'm glad I got my own world, 'cause it look like it's 'bout to be a war on yo' planet."

* * *

"Just be cool, baby," Stone said to Mona as the masked driver pulled him out of the backseat by his arm.

Mona sat in the passenger seat wondering what was next. She didn't know for sure how Roy was going to play the whole thing out. Or which masked man was him for that matter. Figuring the one left in the car with her was Roy, she decided to speak to him, just to ease her mind some.

"So, what y'all 'bout to do now?" she asked, not wanting to

make it obvious that the job was being worked from the inside in case she was left alone with one of Roy's boys.

She got no answer. The man looked to her, then turned away, which gave her the chills. For all she knew, she could've been in the hands of some real outlaws, villains who didn't know her or her cutthroat scheme. Her hands began to sweat as she tried to think of something or someway to let her know if she was with Roy. Before she could muster a complete thought, the passenger door swung open.

"Bring her," said the masked man who went in with Stone. "That nigga ain't actin' right. Bring her!"

"What? Bring me? I don't know nuthin'!" she pleaded, thinking of a possibly painful torture session for her for Stone trying to be hardcore. "Y'all need to let me pee!" She walked so slowly she got a shove from one of the men. The thought of his hoarse whisper to keep his voice hidden gave her the chills. *This ain't Roy or they wouldn't be disguisin' they voices when Stone not around,* she thought as she went through the side door.

Inside, tied to a kitchen chair with blood leaking from his nose and mouth, was Stone.

"Oh, baby!" Mona shrieked in spooked soprano. "What they do to you?"

Stone didn't say a word, just looked to the floor.

"I thought y'all was gon' let me pee?" Mona began to do the bloated-bladder dance.

One of the men pulled her to the bathroom by her arm, undid her cuffs, and stood there as she pissed.

"You could've at least turned around," she said before the cuffs were put back on her.

"Now you see we got your girl in here; don't make us hurt hurt her," the other masked man was saying to Stone in his hoarse whisper as Mona entered the kitchen.

"Man, I don't even know her like that. That's just a bitch I met at the bar. Just some pussy!"

Mona's heart dropped at Stone's words. She couldn't believe he was selling her out like that. She knew she was fucked in the game for sure.

"Damn, it's like that, nigga?" she said to Stone, her words laced with venom as her temper flared. "It's fucked up to be just pussy! I hope they beat yo' ass!"

"I don't know, homeboy," the masked man began. "Sound like she pissed at you. I think some feelin's involved."

Stone sucked his teeth, then looked to the floor again.

"Give 'em the money, damn! I know you got some, and they do, too! Our life is more important than that shit!" Mona screamed. She dared not tell herself, because even if that wasn't the job she planned, it would be a bitch to convince Stone otherwise.

"Listen to yo' woman," one of the men said. "She makin' good sense. You see we got our faces covered, that mean that once we get what we want, we outta here!"

"Fuck y'all!" Stone said.

"Oh, fuck us?" asked the second masked man. "Naw, fuck that pussy you got! That's what you said it was, just pussy, right? Pass the pussy!" he said to his partner.

Mona was shoved from one masked man to the other. The one who caught her pulled her by the arm to the kitchen table, pulled another chair from under it, and pushed her face down into the seat of the chair.

"Stone!" she screamed as her skirt was lifted from behind. Her thong was snatched down before she heard a zipper. She tried to look to see if Roy was the one behind her, but saw no signs to give him away.

"Owww!" escaped her mouth as she was entered from the rear. She began to sob uncontrollably as she was raw-dogged by the mysterious individual, not from pain, but from the fear and frustration of not knowing.

It wouldn't have been so bad to her if she knew for sure Roy was inside her, but she didn't. She didn't even know if this was her set-up, meaning she might not even get paid. On top of it all, she was being hit raw, and had no idea what her assailant might have. Stone didn't seem to give a damn!

"Why you puttin' that girl through all that?" asked the other masked man.

"Fuck her," Stone said.

"Guess you really don't care. Well, I got somethin' for that, too," the masked man said. He pulled Stone out of the chair, then hit him in the gut. When he sat Stone back in the chair, his boy was just finishing with Mona.

"What's goin' on?" asked the rapist.

"This nigga still ain't sayin' nothin'. We gon' have to hurt 'em." He pulled a pair of pruning shears from his back pocket. He tossed the shears to his partner, then put the gun to Stone's head. "I want you to try some slick shit!"

The rapist went to the back of the chair and grabbed Stone's hands. He clipped the first segment of Stone's pinky finger, then picked it up and laid it in Stone's lap.

As Stone screamed, he received a slap in the face. Once he calmed some, he had a sudden change of heart. He told where all the money was, where all the dope and jewelry was, and even where his gators and suits were.

Mona just shook her head. *You coulda did that at first, dummy!*

* * *

Like young boys trading Christmas stories, Johnny and Ross rode home from work talking about all the friendly women on their job. Ross just knew there was no way Johnny's lunch could've matched his, not without the use of the van anyway.

"And then we went out to the car," Johnny said.

"You fuck?" Ross asked, thinking the most that could've happened was for Johnny to be treated to a meal.

"Man, c'mon. This me!"

"Well, the chick I was with be slangin' boy," Ross said like

Santa left him a bike compared to Johnny's skateboard.

"Heroin?" Johnny asked with raised eyebrows.

"Yup. Be servin' the foreman and everything."

"She looked like she was on you."

"She is. Bought us a extra hour for our break."

"That's gravy! You fuck?"

"Naw--"

"Well see, everybody can't be--"

"I got some skull!"

"You lyin'!"

"Nope! Back there in the back. It was A-1, too. Now what was you sayin'? Everybody can't what?"

"Man, fuck you!"

"Don't hate. Oh yeah! I need to get a plug so I can hook up ol' girl."

"Damn, y'all on the grind over in yo' world. My world is laid back. It's a gang of bitches, though."

"Shit, my world is grimy, look like the alley. Niggas be runnin' numbers and shit."

"Damn! Y'all in the gutter. We over in the suburbs. You better get with Stone for that boy. You know he keep a helluva bag.

"Dial his number."

Ross waited as Johnny got no answer from Stone's phone. He wanted to holla at Stone, but wanted to be prepared whenever Felicia was ready to re-up. "He still ain't answer yet?" Ross asked. "I would wait, but I need to get down tonight. Who else you know?"

"I almost forgot about Derek. He had told me he had work when we did that thang at Smurf's."

"Hit 'em up."

"We can just fall through. He at home, probly just watchin' TV or somethin'."

At Derek's, Johnny knocked, but instead of an answer, Derek shouted from inside, "Who is it?"

"Johnny!"

"Go around back; it's open."

"Man, you better stop leavin' yo' door open," Johnny said to Derek once they got inside. "You ain't down South!"

"What y'all into?" Derek asked.

"You still got work?" Ross asked.

"Heron," Derek said.

"I need a small quarter."

Chapter 18

Nearly a month after Johnny started his new job, he and Sonya enjoyed a meal at Union Street. He now had a special cellphone for his women on the side, but told Sonya it was for his hustle. Since he started working, he and Ross only did two jobs. Both were Stone's lieutenants thought to have crossed.

After their meal, Johnny checked his cellphone. He had eight missed calls. It was Friday, Valentine's Day and Nikki wanted a slice of him.

"You gotta take care of some business, baby?" Sonya asked after seeing him check his phone.

"I don't know yet," Johnny lied to keep his options open. "I hope not 'cause I planned to spend the rest of the night with you. To tell you the truth, I'm too tired from work to go out," he said, knowing he spent valuable energy tossing Lynn in Ross's van during his lunchbreak.

"Well, if it's money to be made, I'll understand. Do your thang, baby. I'll be home when you get back."

"It's cool, but we goin' home first."

"I don't know why, you ain't gettin' none," she said with a smile.

"Yeah, okay!"

An hour after sex, Sonya was asleep, so Johnny took her car keys and bounced.

He smoked a joint on the way to Nikki's, already knowing she wanted to be fucked silly from all the dozens of missed calls he'd received that night.

"Damn, Mr. Clean, I thought you was gon' sell a sista out tonight," Nikki said, answering the door wearing nothing but Izzey Miyake.

"You know I gots to see you on a day like this. I wouldn't be able to sleep if I didn't."

"Yeah, you sound good."

He smacked her on the ass as she led him into the bedroom. "I bet it's gon' feel good, too." He popped a Viagra, then stripped.

"Damn, boo, you still hard," she said after an hour of sex.

Snatching his clothes off a bedside chair, he told her, "It'll stay hard as long as I'm with yo' fine ass."

"You know I can't let you leave me like that," she said as she reached for him.

He climbed to his feet. "Naw. I gotta get back home. You tryin' to kill me!"

He drove home to wake Sonya with his still-erect dick.

"I'm sleep, Johnny," Sonya said.

"But it's still Valentine's Day."

"Not no more; it's past twelve."

"You can't be technical on a day like this." He pulled back the covers and got on top of her.

"Where the hell you been?"

"I had to take care of something right quick. What's wrong?"

"Nigga, you smell like perfume! Who you been out fuckin'?" She pushed him off her.

"Cut it out. You know I ain't been doin' nothin'."

"Then why you smell like Izzey Miyake?" She jumped on him trying to bite him.

"Sonya!"

"And you took my car!" she screamed as she slashed his chest with her nails.

He grabbed her by the arms as she struggled and turned her around. He seized her in a bear hug. She tried to stomp his feet as he held her with his left arm, undoing his pants with his right. Unable to drop his pants to his ankles, he pushed her onto the bed and fell on top of her with his pants around his thighs. He tried to shove his still-hard dick into her from behind as she lay on her stomach. She closed her legs and twisted to keep him from hitting his target.

"I don't know why you movin' like that. I can still hit yo' ass!"

"Johnny, you better not!" she said with her mouth muffled by the pillow as she surrendered.

After giving Sonya an angry fuck to calm her some, Johnny rolled over. "You feel better now?"

"I hate you!"

* * *

Elisa sat in her calming bubble bath thinking of the guilty looks she'd been getting from Herb lately. She knew something was wrong. He was definitely hiding something and she hoped for his sakes it wasn't another woman.

Elisa felt so guilty about laying the love cream on him before that she allowed it to partially wear off. He was starting to make his own decisions and do more of what he wanted. She felt good knowing he was still crazy about her, but didn't trust him. He hadn't even given her a report on Johnny and Ross in weeks, and even then he seemed to be lying. She didn't like that and had been thinking about taking his Valentine's Day gift back, and even having second thoughts about giving him another dose of act-right because of it.

Hearing his car pull into the driveway, she leaped from the tub and dashed into the bedroom. With water dripping from her body, she rambled through her stash of poisons and potions until she found what she needed.

She drained the tub, dried herself and started a fresh hot bath for Herb. She heard the front door open and close. As Herb stepped close to the bathroom she slipped her cream under the sink.

"Hey, baby," she began. "Happy Valentine's Day! I got a hot bath started. I know you had a hard day at work, so I'll let you soak by yourself before you join me in the bedroom."

"Aw, you too much, baby!" Herb said. He went into the bedroom to take off his clothes.

Elisa grabbed the cream and scooped about three teaspoons worth into his bath.

As Herb entered the bathroom, she kissed him and stroked his dick. "Don't keep mama waiting too long, baby. You'll get all wrinkly in there. You know where to find me when you get done."

As Elisa stepped from the bathroom, she was once again consumed by guilt. There in the bedroom was a dozen freshly cut roses with a huge box of chocolates. *Awww, that's so sweet,* she thought, but it was too late. Herb was already basting in enough mind-blow to dummy him up for at least six months.

After his bath, Elisa was waiting under the sheets in her sexy lingerie. She had his gift wrapped Movado underneath her pillow.

He walked in with a towel wrapped around him. She snatched it off as he passed.

"I see my baby's feeling frisky tonight," he said.

She flipped back the covers, revealing her peach-colored panty set.

"I like your new outfit," he said.

"Naw, baby, it's your new outfit. I bought it just for you. It's yours along with everything in it."

Herb hopped into the bed grinning like he'd just smoked a bag of happy weed.

Their tongues entered one another's mouths, then passionately slow danced. Herb pulled his mouth away.

"Did you like your gifts, baby?" he asked.

"The flowers were beautiful, and the candy will last till next year as slow as I eat it." She slipped her hand under her pillow and retrieved the watch. "Here you go, sweetie. Hope it fits. This is for treating me so good and being so honest with me." She threw that in at the last minute knowing that the cream should be just kicking in.

Herb paused before even opening his gift. His face looked like he'd just been caught in bed with her sister. "Look, Elisa, I haven't been completely honest with you."

"What do you mean, Herbie?" she said ever-so-sweetly, knowing the juicy stuff was on the way.

"Well, those boys--"

"Who? Ross and Johnny?"

"Yeah. I know I promised you I'd tell you everything about them, but that's not what I did."

Elisa put her fist under her chin as she listened.

"Every since they started, they've been banging women in the plant like crazy!"

"What?!"

"Yeah, baby. I'm sorry for not telling you, but I didn't want them to find out I told."

She took a deep breath, then started slowly. "Now, let me get this straight, you didn't keep your promise to me, your woman! Because you didn't want those boys mad at you?"

"Well--"

"And this has been going on since they started?"

"I'm afraid so."

"Herbie!"

"You gotta understand, baby. I would have to work with

those guys even if they were no longer with Sonya and Gwen. I would still have to see them everyday."

Elisa thought for a long moment. "I guess maybe you have a point, but I'm still not happy about it, Herbie! You promised!"

"I know, baby," he said with a pitiful expression.

"I don't want you to have any problems on your job; that wouldn't be smart at all."

"Now you see!"

"Hold on, Mr. Man! Just hold it right there! What else have you been keeping from me?"

* * *

"Why do it keep goin' soft?" Mona asked Stone while trying to mount him. She had come to meet him at another of his houses to buy dope. She felt so sorry for his finger being snipped that she tried to give him a shot of sympathy ass. But he couldn't keep it up for some reason.

After the robbery incident, he told her to go to the police about her rape so they could gather DNA, but she said she got her period so it would be no proof. Every since, he'd been avoiding her at the bar and everywhere else. And he wouldn't go near his house where he was tied up. She knew he didn't think she was involved or else she would've been a dead body like his former lieutenants.

Mona knew Stone never trusted his top workers, and three days after the set-up went down, they were both found, but their heads weren't.

Mona figured that Stone's limpness was due to him seeing the masked man dog her from behind the way he did, or maybe Stone just didn't feel like the man around her anymore after he knew she witnessed him fold under the torture and get diarrhea of the jaw. Whatever it was, it had to be mental because he was in working order before. She couldn't even suck him stiff.

She bought a big eighth, then caught a cab home.

Mona had purchased the dope from Stone, but didn't really need it yet. She had plenty of dope from the robbery, but had to cop as she did before to keep Stone from getting wise. In a way, she hoped he would just cut her off altogether.

She pulled out her cellphone to call Roy while on her way home. "Hello? Yeah, this Kim."

"Oh, you alright?" Roy asked.

"What you doin'?"

"I'm kind of busy right now," Roy said before hanging up. He'd been acting funny since the robbery, acting like he didn't want to be bothered with Mona either. She knew what the problem was. He had the fifty thousand dollars they stole and lost his appetite for her since he now had so many other chicks due to his flashy behavior. She knew he didn't want her around to keep her from knowing exactly who had the cash.

Three weeks ago, before Mona knew who the masked men were for sure, she called Roy.

"Hey, baby!" he said.

"What happened to you?" she asked, not wanting to let him know that she didn't know if he was in the mask or not.

"Oh, I was gonna call you. I just wanted to wait until everything cooled down some, that's all," he told her.

"Quit bullshittin'! It ain't hot. Wasn't no police called or nothin'!" She was now furious thinking he'd tried to play her out of her cut. "Just fall through tonight; I got you," he told her before hanging up.

That night when she got to his house, no one answered the door, and he wouldn't answer his phone. She called again while standing on his porch and could hear his cellphone ringing inside the house, but still no answer. She knew for sure some shit was in the game.

Two days later, she popped up at Roy's house to see a female running out and hopping into a cab. She ran to the door before he could close it. "Who was that?" she asked.

"Oh, that's my cousin."

Mona immediately noticed a huge gold chain around Roy's neck with a Mickey Mouse charm hanging from it. The rodent's ears were filled with diamond boogers.

Acting as if she didn't see it, she pushed her way into the house. In his bedroom, he had all sorts of new clothes and shoes, things he couldn't afford before.

"What the fuck happened the other night?" she inquired.

"Man, you ain't gon' believe this, but my dog got arrested that night and I was hidin' in a garage so the police couldn't find me."

"Yeah, right!"

"I ain't lyin'! He was tryin' to sell some of the heroin we stole, but the nigga he met was undercover. I got away 'cause I was out in the car."

"So where he at now?" she asked.

"He in the County. I ain't goin' down there to get locked up myself. His people ain't got the cash to get him out."

"So why you ain't just take some money to his people so they can get him out?" she asked, seeing the scurviness in Roy for leaving his dog stankin'.

"Man..." He looked to the floor, unable to answer.

"Okay, where the money at?"

"Ol' boy had--"

"How did I know you was gon' say that?"

"Man, I ain't lyin'! He had the dough and I had the work. If I knew where he hid it, I woulda went and got it already."

"Roy," she began calmly. "If that nigga had the loot, he would've told his people where it was so they coulda bailed him out. And when I asked you why you ain't give 'em the money, you woulda said you ain't have it then!"

"Man, look! I ain't gotta lie to you!"

"Naw, you don't," she said, realizing she should play things cool until she at least got the dope.

"Here, take the dope, and when he get out, I'll tighten you up with the dough."

She opened the duffel bag he handed her and almost cracked a smile. There were ten untouched mushrooms waitin' to be cut for the flippin'. She knew she was going to make a killin' once she did her thang with them.

"This all of it?" she asked, remembering who she was dealing with.

"All except that shit ol' boy got caught with."

"You don't want none of it?" She thought it was strange for him to give it all away even if he did have the cash.

"Man, that nigga bond is a hundred thousand for tryin' to sell that shit. I ain't fuckin' wit' that at all!"

"Oh, so you gon' just give me the hot shit? You skantless as hell!"

As Roy laughed, Mona thought of the way she was bent over at Stone's. She still wasn't sure if Roy was the one who did it after seeing how shiesty he actually was. *I bet yo' skantless ass would let yo' boy fuck me! I should stab yo' ass right now! s*he thought as Roy continued to laugh about dropping the dope on her. She knew he thought he was doing her wrong by even giving her the dope. He had no idea she could move it.

As she turned away, she almost instinctively rolled her eyes, but caught herself. She didn't want him to have any idea how mad she really was 'cause she had plans for him.

Chapter 19

Johnny walked into the breakroom at work and the wonderful aroma of cooked shrimp whirled up his nostrils. He looked around and found Herb at a corner table, smashing a dish of something so delicious he didn't seem to notice Johnny standing over him.

"What you eatin'?" Johnny asked.

"Seafood gumbo," Herb managed between mouthfuls.

Thinking that Herb would offer him some, Johnny took a seat. Herb continued feasting, slurping shamelessly as he sucked the meat from the crableg shells.

"They sell that on the lunch wagon?" Johnny asked, terribly munched out from smoking weed.

"Naw, my baby made this 'specially for me."

"Elisa can cook like that?"

Herb continued with no trace of table manners.

"Damn, Herb! At least let a brotha taste it!"

Herb looked up from his meal. "Grab one of those cups over there."

Johnny jumped up and snatched one of the styrofoam cups and a plastic spoon from the counter. He couldn't wait to get the stuff into his mouth.

"How is it?" Herb asked after Johnny tasted his first spoonful.

Slightly spicy and definitely juicy, a flavor-loaded shrimp busted inside Johnny's mouth as his teeth clamped down on it. He thought that Sonya could burn, but Elisa was obviously the law in the kitchen. A condemned man couldn't make a last request for a better meal before execution. Johnny needed at least a warehouse full of Elisa's grub. "Man, this shit is the bomb. She should be gettin' paid."

"I hope you liked it 'cause I can't come off no more, young fella!"

"Man, tell her I'll pay her to make me a pot of this! Naw, a roaster full! A pot won't be big enough," Johnny said with a greedy smile.

"Johnny," Sonya called two days later. "The phone is for you." She handed him the phone, rolled her eyes and walked away.

"Hello?" he said. "Oh, Herb! What's up, playa?"

"I told Elisa what you said, and she made enough gumbo for you, Derek and Ross. Of course she won't take any money from you, 'cause you're in the family."

"Oh, cool. Cool!"

"Do you have Ross's number handy?"

"Aw, man, don't even worry about it. I'll give Ross and Derek theirs. I'll be right over."

Later that night, Johnny sat at the dining room table, hunched over a heaping bowl of gumbo. Sonya sat watching.

"Is it really that good?" she asked in a jealous tone.

Johnny nodded with a smile. "Want some?"

"No thanks. I had enough growing up."

Once he got back into his bowl Sonya sucked her teeth and stormed out of the room. He didn't make a move after her. He didn't care; he had his gumbo along with a few scoops from Ross and Derek's dishes. He was straight!

After wolfing the gumbo until he looked to be nearing his third trimester, he headed for the bedroom. Sonya was laying across the bed in her sexiest nightie. Johnny ignored her, shucked his clothes and got into bed.

"You just gon' go to sleep?" she asked.

"I thought you was mad at me." He felt his head hit the pillow, then heard Sonya shouting his name.

"What? Why you yellin' like that?"

"'Cause you act like you can't hear! You 'bout to be late for work."

"I just laid down."

"Johnny you been sleep since last night. The alarm clock went off thirty minutes ago!"

He jumped up, showered, then slipped on his clothes.

Outside as he waited for his ride, Johnny discovered that Ross was running late also.

"Man, that gumbo was out cold!" Ross said when he finally arrived.

"Hell yeah. Ol' girl can cook her ass off!" Johnny said.

"I can't wait till Elisa make some more of that shit."

* * *

With Stone pretty much out of her life, Mona concentrated her efforts on Smurf. He had been hounding her for a date or anything he could get out of her.

Derek had been back out in the streets hustling since he was healed, so Mona dug Smurf's number out of her purse.

"What's up?" Smurf said once he found out it was Mona calling him.

"I was just calling like I promised to. What you into?"

"Tryin' to get next you. Is that possible?"

"We can talk about it."

"Well, let's get together. We can grab a bite to eat or somethin'. It's five now. What time do you go to work?"

"I don't work today. Where we goin'?" she asked as she practiced her Kegels.

"It don't matter. You want me to come get you?"

"You know I still live with my man. I'll meet you somewhere."

At club Celebrity, Mona ordered a catfish platter, but didn't really have an appetite. Every time she looked at Smurf, she could only think of the way he tried to kill Derek. "So what you do for a living, Mr. Smurf?"

"I own a record shop over on Fenkell."

"Runnin' your own business. That's good. I need to get a job so I can leave that bar alone," Mona said, hoping Smurf would let her deep enough into his world for her to put together another scheme. She knew from Derek that Smurf pushed work, and she figured that somehow she could find a way to get into his pockets before killing him.

"I need a cashier, but I know that don't compare to the money you make at the bar," he told her.

"It's a start to get me out the bar. I'm ready to leave that shit alone."

"That's a good attitude to have. I can show you the shop when we leave here."

At the shop, Mona could tell Smurf was sloppy by the way he allowed his crew to hang out in front. They were all dopeman fresh with rimmed up whips.

Some immediately recognized Mona from the bar and spoke. She was glad she never tricked with any of them, knowing it might've complicated things as far as her getting close to Smurf.

"So, is this where I'll be working?" Mona asked as she passed a deserted cash register. A frail but cute girl stood behind the other register looking at Mona like she wanted her dead.

"Yeah, pretty much, but let me show you around first."

When they got to Smurf's office, Mona looked around for any signs of drug activity, but only saw a stuffed garbage bag in the corner. "It smell like weed in here," she lied, hoping he might somehow give himself away.

"Do it?" he asked. "I think I smoked a joint in here earlier."

"Naw, not weed smoke. More like a pine smell. Like a lotta weed."

Smurf looked nervous, but played it off. "I don't know what that could be. Let me light one of these incense sticks to kill whatever it is you smell."

"That's a good idea," she said.

"So, what you think?" Smurf asked.

"It's okay. It's a job; that's the most important thing."

"When can you start?"

"Tomorrow!"

"That's good and bad," Smurf said.

"What's bad about it?"

"I don't mess around with my workers. That's no good for business."

"So it's either or?" Mona played along, knowing he was lying from the cashier's lethal stare.

"Yup. That's the only way I can do it."

"Well, that's too bad for us, 'cause I really need to get out the bar." Mona knew if there was just an affair with Smurf, she could've wound up screwed without the needed info to work her plan. But being in his shop gave her better access to his world, to the things most jump-off broads never get to know or see. Since she knew he had a thing for her, she knew she could get more leverage once she found a way to get him to break his own code and bend her over his desk. And once she decided to do her thang, the cute-faced stick at the register wouldn't stand a chance.

* * *

"Why you actin' funny?" Felicia asked Ross.

For the last few days, he didn't feel much like being bothered with her, and she was pissed about it.

"I ain't actin' funny; I'm just chillin'," Ross told her.

"You must got another bitch up in here somewhere!" Felicia said as she stepped close and put a finger in Ross's face.

Felicia quickly dropped her finger as Ross checked her with a look. "I don't care how mad you get, don't do that shit no more," he said.

She sweetened her tone. "Why you gotta act like that? We ain't cool no more?"

"We cool, I just don't feel like bein' bothered." He turned and walked away.

With forty-five minutes left on their lunch break, Ross and Johnny met at the van to smoke a blunt.

"Man, Felicia been trippin' lately," Ross said.

"Yeah, I been havin' the same problems with Nikki and Lynn. Bitches act like I gotta fuck 'em everyday or somethin'. They know I got a woman. I don't even return Nikki's calls no more."

They drove to a nearby hamburger joint and as they were leaving the drive-thru, Johnny looked into his side mirror. "That's that snake-faced mu'fucka that robbed me and Derek at the afterhour a while back!"

"What you wanna do?" Ross asked. He wasn't as enthused as he usually would be about gettin' some get-back like that, but figured he was just tired from working.

"Man, fuck that nigga! That shit went down months ago. Let's just get back to work."

Ross couldn't believe Johnny was giving the dude a pass. Normally, he would've been out of the van with both feet in snake-face's ass.

Back on the job, Ross stood on his platform, busy at work while Felicia walked over.

"I apologize for gettin' mad earlier. I was wrong," she said.

"It ain't nothin', we still cool."

"So, you still gon' hook me up?"

"Yeah, you know I got you. I ain't mad at you or nothin'. I just don't feel like doin' it right now."

"That's good, 'cause I'm gon' need to re-up tomorrow. And I'll be ready for you whenever you feel like it again, baby."

Chapter 20

Two weeks after Johnny saw snake-face at the fast food joint, Johnny was taking the trash out to the dumpster and saw Mrs. Brooks, one of his neighbors.

Mrs. Brooks was ancient as prostitution. Gray-haired with skin baggy as old man nuts, she was a devout Christian and toted her bible everywhere she went. Her mind was an archive of remedies and wise sayings.

"Hello, Johnny," she said.

Johnny said, "Hi," and kept going.

"Hey, Johnny," she called. "Can I talk to you for a second?"

He dropped the bags and walked back to her. "What's goin' on, Mrs. Brooks?"

"Are you feelin' okay?"

"Yeah, I'm okay. Why you ask?"

"I've noticed a change in you lately."

"How's that?" he asked.

"You used to hang out and come in at all times of the night, but now you just go to work and come back home. You never even leave unless it's to that dumpster or to work."

Johnny was confused. *Damn, I guess she right! It's like leavin' don't even cross my mind no more!* He stood speechless, wondering how she was able to tell the difference when he hadn't noticed it himself.

"Listen, dear, I want you to go and see a friend of mine." She fetched a small piece of paper in her pocket that must've had the address written on it and handed it to him. "She'll be expecting you. You don't have to pay her anything. Just leave a twenty-dollar donation if you feel better after you see her."

"You tryin' to say somethin' is wrong with me?" he asked. He was starting to get scared as he thought of the viral outbreak that occurred some years earlier.

"Yes, I think something is wrong. You might not be able to see it, but it's there." She turned and walked back into her apartment.

For the rest of that day, Johnny couldn't think of anything but what the old woman said. He couldn't place the time that the change happened, but when he thought about it enough, he didn't touch other women, go out, or drink anymore. He couldn't even remember the last time he felt like doing anything outside of work or the apartment.

"Sonya," he said later that day.

"What's up?" she said. She was in bed wrapped in the covers, watching a movie.

"Do I seem different to you?"

"How do you mean?"

"Like the way I act and stuff."

"Oh, that! Yeah, I know what you talkin' 'bout."

"Huh? You know?"

"Yeah, I love it, too!" She pulled back the covers, and with lovey-dovey eyes she held out her arms like she was a boy-crazy teenager. "Come here and watch this movie with me."

Johnny flashed back on the last few weeks and realized why she was acting so weird.

She was happy! He hadn't just been in the apartment lately, but he'd been in there bangin' Sonya three or four times a day. It was happening so much that neither of them bothered to put clothes on while at home. And when he wasn't inside her, she was wrapped around him some kind of way while they watched TV.

"Hold on! I'm tryin' to find out what's wrong with me."

"Ain't nothin' *wrong!* And stop talkin' like it's a bad thang! Ain't nothin' wrong with gettin' older and wantin' to settle down some."

As soon as she said the word "settle", Johnny knew she had marital thoughts racing through her mind. "I was talkin' to Mrs. Brooks today, and she could even tell somethin' was wrong with me." He was now frustrated because Sonya didn't seem to care.

"Since when do you talk to Mrs. Brooks? I be'not find out you and that old woman got somethin' goin' on. She'll get the beatdown!"

Oh, now she got jokes! He thought as he gave up on trying to talk to her about it. He knew that she knew what she liked, so he knew there was no talking to her about his change at all. Somebody or something snuck him, and she was loving every minute of it.

Hating that he had to wait until the next day to go see Mrs. Brooks's friend, he tried to remember what was so fabulous about the streets that always drew him to them. The thing that got him the most was how he somehow missed the memo on the majestic treatments that were in the place where he lived. He was being pampered by a fine-ass sex slave.

Johnny almost lost his balance as he danced out of his pants. *This might not be so bad after all!*

* * *

Mona grabbed her purse and keys before going out to work.

She looked at Derek who was contently watching TV. She took a deep breath and went over to kiss him.

A week ago, he'd bought her a car to get back and forth to work in. It was a six-year old Toyota Camry, but it ran good and had low mileage. The surprise came on her birthday, and he even made sure he picked her favorite color. She loved it.

When Derek was hitched to the shit-bag, Mona would tell him he was only staying out of the streets because he was injured. But now, he was all better and seemed to avoid the streets as much as possible.

Their arguments stopped, and he didn't even question her about where she was going when she went out. He still spoiled her and smothered her with affection. The bundles of roses were common, but not regular enough to drive away her excitement over them. The floor of her closet was insulated by the various designer shoes he'd buy her when he really wanted to thrill her. She loved shoes.

"What was that for?" he asked.

Mona put her hand on her hip. "Can't I kiss my man?"

"Yeah. Wasn't nothin' wrong with it. It was just so soft and smooth, like you wanna get chased into the room or somethin'."

"Maybe later. I gotta get to work." She turned and headed for her car.

Since it was Thursday, Mona knew that her co-worker, the cute-faced stick, had the day off, so she wore her shortest skirt with a shirt cut so low that a cough might've caused a wardrobe malfunction. She knew that at closing time she and Smurf would be there alone and she planned to paralyze his discipline and self-control long enough to get where she needed to be. She would always catch him looking at her, and tonight he was going to go home with his nose open wide enough for his brains to roll out.

Mona sashayed past Smurf as he talked to a guy he knew. She could feel the men's eyes lock on her as she switched. She went to the register she worked and watched as Smurf was handed a gym bag.

"Mona," Smurf called. "Could you take this to my office?"

Mona took her time as she carried the bag, trying to swing or shake it as much as possible to detect the contents. As she placed the bag on Smurf's desk, she gripped it around the sides and felt dozens of folded wads of paper. It had to be money.

Before closing time, Mona saw four more men bring bags to Smurf which were stashed in his office. Some were larger and some smaller than the first.

"Lock all the doors," Smurf told her at closing time.

Doing as she was told, Mona locked the doors, then counted the money from her drawer. She watched as Smurf closed the door that led to the hallway where his office door was. She knew he was up to something. She never saw that door closed before.

Curious as a doomed feline, she went through the door Smurf had closed and saw that his office door was closed also. She went into the restroom, wiggled out of her skirt, then pulled her top over her head. Stepping out of her panties, she placed everything on top of the closed toilet seat.

Covered by nothing but her high heels and pubic triangle, she barged into Smurf's office.

"Hey," Smurf said as he jumped out of his chair. He was behind his desk counting a mountain of cash. "What you--" His eyes scoured Mona's naked body.

Doing her runway walk, she moved close to him and grabbed his hand. She placed it over one of her tits and stabbed his palm as her nipple perked. Leaving his hand over her breast, she reached and undid his sagging jeans. They fell to the floor and out sprang a dick that was harder than Chinese arithmetic.

"Since you busted up in here, you gon' have to help me count this money!"

"We can do that later!"

Chapter 21

"My name is Johnny. Mrs. Brooks sent me," Johnny said as he waited at the door of a small loft a block away from Tiger Stadium. The door swung open and Johnny looked back at Sonya's small Honda as if it were his last time seeing it.

Fragile, with a bandanna cloaking her hair, an elderly woman stepped from behind the door. "Come in, son," she said in a creaky voice.

Johnny looked around at the loft's interior. It was a museum, displaying the joys of the woman's livelier days. Timeworn black and white pictures decorated the walls, while everything else, including the furniture seemed to be antiques.

After closing the door, the old woman said, "Yes, you're a very bad case. Could you please take off your right shoe?"

"My right shoe?" Johnny asked.

"Yes, please." The woman pulled a small piece of paper from in between her tea-bag titties. She handed it to Johnny.

"Place this in your shoe."

Johnny looked at the paper. It was a passage from the book of Psalms. He did as he was told.

"Now put your shoe back on."

Johnny stood in the middle of the floor as the woman went to the upper section of the loft and returned with a tambourine.

"Close your eyes, son."

"Johnny heard a match strike, then inhaled the aroma of incense. He could hear the tambourine rattling high and low as the woman circled him singing a hymn. Johnny clamped his eyes tight while his forehead was anointed with something wet that ran down his face and dribbled off his nose. *This is crazy!*

"Keep your eyes closed," the woman began. "I want you to recite the Lord's Prayer with me."

After the recitation, Johnny could hear the floor creak as the woman walked around him.

"Okay, son. You can open your eyes now."

As Johnny lifted his eyelids, it felt as if a lampshade was removed from his head. His thoughts were clearer and he felt full of energy. It was like a portion of his mind was somehow clouded before.

He turned to the woman, she appeared twenty years younger.

"Thanks," he said as he went into his pocket. He pulled out a roll of bills and peeled off a hundred. "I don't know what you did, or what was wrong with me, but thanks!"

Thinking of how silly he would sound to Ross, Johnny wondered if he should tell him at all. Instead, he floored the Honda, pointing it in the direction of Nikki's apartment.

* * *

Still naked except for a pair of rubber gloves, Mona had been counting an hour before she put a dent in Smurf's mountain of money. She was now at three hundred-thousand and from the looks of things, she had at least two hours to go.

"I just know I got a raise comin'," Mona said to Smurf who

was sitting in the corner naked with a joint and a cup of gin trying to regain his vitality after Mona's pussy attack.

"You high as you can go! I manage the place myself."

"Nigga, I ain't countin' all this damn money for free!"

"I know. I'm gon' throw you a gee' for that. And tomorrow, after I hook up, I'm gon' need you to help put the bags together for my team. That's another gee'."

"That's what I'm talkin' about! What kind of work you be handlin' anyway?"

"Just weed. I don't need to do nothin' else. I would put you on with a few pounds, but I don't know if you can work it."

"Yeah, right! Every nigga I know sell weed. I know you gon' give me a gravy ticket so I can get 'em off like hotcakes."

"I'll give you three for nine hundred apiece."

With a hand on her hip, Mona said, "Guess you ain't like this pussy!"

"Since you put it like that, I might be able to work five at eight-fifty."

Thinking of Smurf's ten strokes before he came, she knew she could write her own ticket. "What about ten to start with, at eight hundred apiece?"

"You squeezin' me!"

Sweetening her voice, Mona said, "You know I'm gon' let you squeeze me back." Slipping off the rubber gloves, she walked over and fondled Smurf's dick until it was semi-erect.

"Alright, I'm gon' see what you can do, but I don't want no sob stories if somethin' go wrong!"

As Smurf's eyes rolled back in his head to the tune of Mona's massaging hand, she looked down at his exposed neck with murderous thoughts. She wondered if Derek was told, "no sob stories" before he was shot.

After the cash was counted, Mona hopped in her ride and pulled off. She dialed Roy Jr. to see if he had any new bullshit to tell her.

"Hey, what's up, baby!"

"Why you sound so happy to hear from me? You wasn't tryin' to be bothered before," Mona said.

"Then why you still callin' me?"

"Oh, you gettin' smart, nigga? See if I call yo' ass again!"

"Wait! I was just bullshittin' with you. You know I miss you," Roy said.

That nigga's money must be gettin' low!

"Why you gettin' all mad anyway? Must be that time of the month."

"Naw, for yo' information it ain't! And don't be tryin' to check anyway; it ain't like you hittin' nothin!"

"Man, I ain't tryin' to beef with you or nothin'."

"Where the rest of my money then?"

"Ol' boy still ain't got out yet. You know that."

"Well, I got a way you can make up for it and get paid, too."

"You got another lick set up?"

"Somethin' like that. But this time you gon' have to kill the nigga. Oh yeah, kill the little skinny bitch workin' the cash register, too!"

Chapter 22

"What the hell you want?" Nikki said to Johnny as she stood in her T-shirt holding her front door open.

"What's all that for?" he asked. "I ain't know we was beefin'."

"I'm just sayin', you ain't wanna come over when I was askin' you to. Why you comin' now? Yo' woman told you she got a headache?"

"That's funny. You gon' let me in?"

"You don't deserve to come in here, Mr. Clean. You kicked me to the curb. I ain't like the way you played me."

"I wasn't feelin' right."

"What you mean, you wasn't feelin' right?"

"It's hard to explain. Just let me in and I'll try to explain it better."

"No, I don't want to let you in, 'cause you hurt my feelin's. And I know if I let you in, you just gon' be tryin' to get some."

"I promise not to even try to get none unless you

understand. Okay?"

"No, Mr. Clean! Just leave everything like it is. You got a woman anyway. If I start back fuckin' with you, I'm gon' be the one to get hurt. Not you! You just want to fuck!"

The whole time Nikki was talking, Johnny was scoping out her creamy thighs. Her shirt was just low enough to keep him from seeing her bush. But he knew what treasures were beneath her shirt and thinking about them made his dick throb.

Realizing she was being undressed by Johnny's eyes, Nikki stepped behind the door, out of his horny view.

Seeing that there was no reasoning with her, Johnny pushed the door open.

"Boy," Nikki shouted as she danced her bare feet away from the swinging door.

Johnny stepped inside and slammed the door. He turned to Nikki who was backing away as if she were being stalked by a werewolf.

"Gone, Mr. Clean! I don't feel like playin'!"

"That's 'cause you ain't had none in a while."

"I thought you was just gon' explain what was wrong with you?"

"I will when you stop tryin' to get away!"

"Naw, 'cause you think you slick!"

With a fluid hand movement, Johnny seized Nikki's wrist and pulled her into his embrace. He threw her over his shoulder like she was a shirt.

Nikki's feet dangled as she was carried into her bedroom and dropped to a bounce on her bed. "I hate you!"

Johnny yanked off his coat and eased his body onto Nikki's. Resting on his elbows, he looked into her eyes. He could see that she was only mad at him, that she wanted him there.

She twisted her head in a stank way while still maintaining eye contact as if she wanted to ask, "What you lookin' at?"

In the few moments that Johnny lay face to face with Nikki, he could feel the extent of her pain, the loneliness he created by spinnin' her off. He realized that her pain wouldn't be righted by a simple explanation, so he decided to keep his story of invisible lampshades and wrinkly women with high-powered perception.

Johnny doubted Nikki had panties on, and knew penetration was a mere push away. But he also realized that if he wanted her to give it up, to want him to have her again and actually pump back, he would have to get back inside her head. He needed to pour out his feelings and tell her the real reason he couldn't cut her loose and had to have her love at least four times a week.

The gazing into Nikki's pupils went on for less than two minutes that felt to Johnny like eons. He knew she was giving him time to do what he needed to and bring her back into a fold of his world where she so desperately felt the need to be.

After mentally devising a helluva line to reel her back in, he opened his mouth to speak, but the words were no longer there. He slowly shook his head. “I miss you, Nikki,” fell from his mouth before he could close it.

Wanting to have said something with a little more thug in it, he was shocked by the way his heart played him.

Nikki looked paralyzed as she scrutinized Johnny's face. Her lips slightly parted, then her eyes pooled with tears. As she looked up at him, a single drop escaped her eye socket and disappeared into her hair.

Johnny stroked her cheek with the back of his fingers, then dropped his mouth to hers. He pressed passion into her lips with his and captured her face with his hands.

Lifting his head, he told her, “Please believe I care about you. I hope you forgive me for neglectin' you like I did. It was all my fault, you ain't do nothin' wrong. If I could go back to the last time I was with you, I wouldn't be able to change the things that went on with me while we was apart. It was just like that, but I take full responsibility 'cause I know I was the one that got your heart involved in this in the first place. I got other stuff goin' on, but if you can find it deep inside--where the blood and guts is—to forgive me, I promise I won't let you down...not ever!"

Nikki's lids eclipsed her eyes as she slowly nodded in submission.

Johnny once again lowered his mouth to her sublime lips. Allowing her tongue to conquer his in a rousing battle, he propped himself up with his right hand and undid his pants with his left. Her hands slid under his shirt and down into his draws, bringing them down enough to free his wood.

Nikki's legs parted like a reflex when Johnny reached down to slide his pants lower. Her hands drifted up Johnny's back with his shirt, taking it over his head, throwing it on the floor. As he nestled between her parted legs, he spilled his tongue back into her mouth. Her legs locked around his. Holding him in a bearhug, she pulled herself up his magnificence, as to say, he wasn't sinking into her fast enough.

As she was bottom-out, she rotated her pelvis and their tongues continued a sticky slow-groove.

With her eyes closed, Nikki's face reflected dramatic pleasure as Johnny slow-rolled her with the finesse of a gigolo turning a million-dollar date.

After coming twice without going soft, Johnny began to wonder if the old woman's cure was having some kind of impact on his pipe laying. Hoping whatever happened to him would last until he was at least ninety, he flipped Nikki over and finished her from behind.

Chapter 23

Mona walked into the record shop on her day off. She was there to assist Smurf in the distribution of his work. She checked her watch and saw that she had an hour before Roy Jr. was scheduled to show.

Walking past her skinny co-worker, Mona grimmed her, waiting for her to do something to piss her off.

The stick rolled her eyes.

"You got some kind of problem with me, bitch?" Mona asked.

"Who you callin' a bitch? Bitch!"

Mona slapped the stick, causing her to fall back into the register.

Smurf ran to separate the women. "Y'all need to chill out! This is a business! Mona, get in my office!"

Mona smirked at the stick as she strutted into Smurf's office.

Smurf went in behind Mona and closed the office door.

"What the fuck is y'all doin'? You know I got all this work in here today. I can't have that kind of shit goin' on!"

"She started it! And anyway, I ain't know you had the work yet. I thought we was still waitin' for you to hook up with yo' people."

"Naw, I already got down. What I need you to do is take these duffel bags to my crew." Smurf gave Mona list of cellphone numbers with the amount of work each individual was due. "Call each one and take them their order, one at a time. You don't have to say your name or nothin'. They all waitin' but don't know who's gon' drop it off. Pull your car to the back door and load your trunk. I got other orders to fill."

Mona pulled her car to the alley exit of the record shop, then grabbed the first duffel bag. She took it home and dropped it in her garage. She repeated that until she got to the last one.

As Mona pulled off with the last bag, she looked into her rear-view mirror to see Roy Jr. darting into the record shop. She laughed to herself, then blasted E-40's "Trump Change" on her sound system.

"...Well, I'm afraid that you no longer have a job," a detective told Mona as she sat in Derek's living room. He was there to interview her since she was the only living person who had anything to do with the record shop.

"Damn!" Mona faked. "I sure am glad I wasn't there!"

The following day, Mona went to Stone to re-up.

"I'm telling you, this nigga got the same heroin you be havin'. He was tryin' to sell me a hundred grams for five gees'."

"For five gees'?" Stone asked. His anger was beginning to show as his chubby face turned red.

"That's why I think he got yo' shit! You don't have to believe me, I'm just tellin' you what I know. And I ain't never seen nobody with the quality you got 'cept this nigga. You ain't gon' sell no A-1 that damned cheap! Think about it!"

As Stone sat in silence for a minute, Mona knew she was getting in his head.

"Why you just ain't cop from the nigga and come up? That's what I woulda did," Stone said with a curious look.

"I don't give a fuck how cheap that shit is, I ain't spendin' no dough with that punk that raped me! I would rather tell you, and if you gon' do somethin' for me, cool. If not, then it's still cool! I just hope you handle yo' biz with them niggas!"

"Alright, dig, where you say the nigga at?"

* * *

"You ready to do that job for Stone?" Johnny asked Ross on the way home from work, Two days had passed since Smurf's death, and even though Johnny had been back to tossin' Nikki and Lynn, he stayed home with Sonya a lot more than before.

"Naw, man. You go ahead. I ain't feelin' that shit right now," Ross told him.

"Man, listen. I wasn't sure if I should tell you this before, but now I know exactly what happened to us."

"What you mean?"

"Elisa put the whammy on us with that gumbo. That had to be it!"

"You crazy as a mu'fucka! I don't think she into no shit like that."

"Nigga, think about how sprung Herb's ass is! He probly wasn't like that before she put the shit on him. You know what they say 'bout women from down there."

"Man, Gwen wouldn't play me like that!"

"I don't think our chicks knew. Sonya was just happy 'cause I was in the crib fuckin' her all day. Think about it for a minute. You don't do nothin' else but work."

Ross got quiet, then started to laugh.

"You gotta go by Derek's tonight, right?"

"Yeah, I need some more dope."

"Okay, let's try to get him out the house. He ain't gon' go, 'cause she got him, too!"

At Derek's, Mona walked back to the couch after letting Johnny and Ross in, then lifted Derek's arm around her neck, snuggling close.

"What's up, cuzo?" Derek asked.

"Wanna hit the bar tonight?" Johnny asked. "Drinks on me!" He knew Derek couldn't resist a buzz at another's expense.

Mona lifted her head and looked at Johnny like he accused her of smelling like fish.

"Naw, man. I'm straight," Derek began. "I don't fuck around no more."

Ross looked to Johnny with raised eyebrows.

"Don't be tryin' to drag mines out in them streets," Mona interjected.

"Oh, we ain't mean no harm, family member," Ross said.

"Okay, 'cause he doin' just fine where he at!" she continued.

"I got this, baby," Derek told Mona. "Grab that package I put together for Ross."

As Mona walked out of the living room, she kept her eyes on Johnny while telling Derek, "That's right, boo. Stay strong. Don't let 'em get you in no trouble!"

"What's the deal, homie?" Ross asked Derek.

"I'm straight. Just chillin'. I don't feel like that shit no more. I'm really thinkin' 'bout gettin' married. Gettin' Herb to plug me with a job down there with y'all."

Ross took a deep breath. "I hear ya, baby. Ain't nothin' wrong with it. Do yo' thang!"

Mona came back, gave Ross the dope, then put the money in her pocket. She resumed her post next to her boo. "Y'all can just slam the door behind y'all," she shouted as the troublemakers left.

"That shit was amazin'!" Ross told Johnny back in the van.

"I told you."

"How you get the shit up off you?"

"Well, it's this old lady, right? You take a donation..."

Later that night, Johnny parked Ross's Impala two streets over from his target's home. Dressed in Sonya's denim skirt and hooded windbreaker, Johnny lifted the hood over his head and walked to Roy Jr.'s door. He knocked, then waited after hearing footsteps from the inside.

"Who is it?" a male voice asked from inside the door.

"Roy?" Johnny asked.

"Who dat?"

"It's me, nigga!"

"Me who?"

"Nigga, quit bullshittin'!"

The door swung open.

Johnny pulled Ross's silenced .45. With the webbing between his forefinger and thumb over the lemon squeeze, he strangled the gat until the clip was spent.

"You handle the nigga?" Stone asked Johnny the following night.

"Yup!" Due to the weather, Johnny had on his large trench coat that hung down slightly over his hands.

"What about the bitch?" Stone asked.

"Fo' sho'!"

Johnny watched as Stone reached under the cushion of the chair he was in and yanked out a small stack of bills. As Johnny leaned over to receive his pay, he slid his knife down his sleeve and sank it into Stone's neck. Johnny twisted his face as the blood squirted from Stone's jugular vein.

"Why did you kill Stone, too?" Ross asked Johnny on their lunchbreaks the following day.

"He wanted me to kill Mona."

"Damn! We woulda been through with pussy!"

"Right!"

"But you know that nigga was a straight up meal ticket."

"Fuck it, man. I don't really want to kill no more anyway. It's like I'm still different after the old woman helped me. I still got my ho's on the side, but I don't really feel all that wild shit no more."

"I feel you. That's why I'm glad I got the 'boy' spinnin' at the job."

"Yeah, that's cool. I think I'm gon' take over the numbers game down here," Johnny said as he rubbed his chin.

"What about Derek? You ain't gon' put him up on game?"

"No. He cool just like he is. Maybe now he'll stay out of trouble. But, I'm still gon' holla if I see that snake-faced mu'fucka again!"

The End

Street Ink Publications Order Form:

Quantity	Book	Price
	Drug Lords	$12.99
	Children of The Night	$12.99
	Shipping & Handling (add $2.50 per book)	
	TOTAL	$

Please make checks payable to Street Ink Publications and send to the following:

Street Ink Publications
15740 W. 7 Mile #1600
Detroit, MI 48235

Please allow four to six weeks for delivery. Most orders shipped immediately.

Name____

Address______________________________________

City, State, Zip________________________________

Phone# (_____)_______________________________

Email: _____________________________________

Other books by this author:

http://streetinkbooks.com

Please visit the website to leave comments and keep up with more of this author's works.